Quotes from those who have read *Southern Winds*:

Ernest Vandiver

Adjutant General, State of Georgia, 1948-1954; Lt. Governor, State of Georgia, 1954-1958; Governor, State of Georgia, 1959-1963

I found *Southern Winds* to be a very interesting book and could not put it down until I read it cover to cover. I was impressed with the way the book is written. There are so many people whom I knew and events in the book of which I had knowledge.

This was a very difficult time period in the South for racial problems, with lawsuits, riots and the beginnings of integration in the schools. While I was Governor, the courts ruled that the Legislature had one year to desegregate the Georgia schools. I was particularly concerned that Georgia not be embarrassed, as some of the other southern states had been. It was my goal to find ways of complying with the law as safely and as smoothly as possible.

Over 200 years of habits of the mind were difficult to change overnight. For some, this was easier than for others. I went before the General Assembly and made an impassioned plea for understanding and compliance with the newly enacted laws. Although I received many threats against my life for doing so, I knew that I had done the right thing. I am proud to say that this was accomplished in our state with only a modicum of disturbances.

In the quest for knowledge and understanding purposes about this era, I feel that this book could serve as required reading and educational.

Hans G. Tanzler

Attorney; former Criminal Court Judge; former Mayor of Jacksonville, Florida

Surely the most divisive enigma facing America today is racial preju-dice and disharmony in all its forms, black and white. With the popu-larization of *Roots*, we have been given a great insight into the past and thus a better understanding of the present.

This fascinating book paints a sensitive picture of life for one white family in a small Georgia town before, during and after integration. A thought provoking flip side that is equally deserving of compassion and consideration in our rush to judgment.

Compulsory reading for all who seek understanding.

Ray Francis Bernardo
Who's Who of the World; Former owner of Providence Granite, Hardwood Island, Maine and hotel in Naraganset Bay, Rhode Island; Member of the Board of Directors of the First Bank and Trust, Providence, Rhode Island

Having lived the role of a Yankee in Providence, Rhode Island, I had no idea of the changes that developed in the South.

With the touch of the writer's pen, and listening to the voice of a southern gentleman, I have gained a much better understanding. There really was another side to the story that I have never read because it hasn't been told. *Southern Winds* has explained the con-flicts that arose, the changes that were forced and reluctance in accepting them.

It is a collection of the author's memoirs.

Dr. Sara West
Expert in Education and Psychology, Palm Beach, Florida

Your style is entertaining. Your voice is sincere as you tell how one white southern gentleman reacted to forced integration. As I read, I understand your pride in your family heritage and your accomplishments.

Your use of dialect is charming, your ear for black dialect is good.

MG (Ret) Joseph W. Griffin
Retired Major General

Many thanks for the look-see at your book. It is good, and articulates many things that thousands, no millions of white folk feel. Best expression I have ever seen or heard.

You have done something I've not read from any other fair-minded, non-bigoted southern white male. That is conveying and spelling out the frustrations we feel and the current hate and hostility that is shown by so many of our black neighbors. It would be good for well-meaning folk of all ethnic groups to read the thoughts you convey in *Southern Winds* and consider them along with those who differ, as well as those who preach hatred.

Dianne Kavanaugh Webb

Thank you for the privilege and the joy you have accorded me, by allowing me the honor of reading your manuscript.

I am a 57-year-old "southern girl" who has shared many of your life's experiences, having been raised in the South. Your book brought tears and laughter to me. I envy you, your ability to so beautifully and in-depth describe your evolving life and feelings.

I am also grateful you acknowledged your Christian heritage, as this is one we share also.

Many good wishes for your success in getting *Southern Winds* published.

Ben Bragman

I thoroughly enjoyed reading your book about growing up as a southerner, through southern "eyes." As a northerner, raised in metropolitan New York, and years spent in rural New Jersey, our lifestyles could not have been more opposite. Most striking to me was your attitude, your reactions and stories involving "black people."

I had little, if any, contact or knowledge of black people outside of a few years when I taught school in Harlem. This book gave me a better understanding of the changes in the South, and the reactions of both races to those changes.

Thank you for giving me the opportunity to read your excellent book.

Pat D. Brooks

When I read *Southern Winds* my mind took a trip back to our childhood together on Williams Street. Our parents would not, in the farthest stretch of the imagination, have imagined all the changes since W.W. II. Life is so-o-o full of good and bad—all interesting. I think of the saying, "Change is not always progress."

Everett, you wrote this book well; you put my thoughts on those pages. I want my children and grandchildren to have the chance to read *Southern Winds*.

Southern Winds

To
Edith Hall,
Please enjoy my
touch of southern
American history
We shared many pages
of this book

Everett Beal

Southern Winds

W. Everett Beal

Writer's Showcase presented by *Writer's Digest*
San Jose New York Lincoln Shanghai

Southern Winds

Published by Writer's Showcase presented by *Writer's Digest*
an imprint of iUniverse.com, Inc.

For information address:
iUniverse.com, Inc.
620 North 48th Street
Suite 201
Lincoln, NE 68504-3467
www.iuniverse.com

ISBN: 0-595-10081-3

Printed in the United States of America

To Judy, my wife and friend

Table of Contents

Foreword

"I have just finished reading *Southern Winds* and am struck with what a compelling social history of the South it is. The bit about the runaway coffin reminded me of Faulkner's, *As I Lay Dying*.

As an English woman who has lived in the South since the middle fifties, I could not help comparing your memories with my own of England in the twenties and thirties. Certainly there was no black and white problem, ours was class, which, if anything, was more rigid than race. World War II did away with a good deal of the divide, but remnants are still there.

Thanks for giving me the opportunity to read your remarkable book."

Bettine Joy Krause
Author
Auburn, Alabama

Preface

The night was black as Egypt. There was no moon; no streetlights to dispel the darkness that was broken only by the glow of small lights that had been left on inside the stores and doctors' offices on the street outside my pharmacy.

I was trying to rest behind the same prescription counter where I had just worked ten hours. There had been no time during the day to get off my feet, and as I lay there I massaged my legs to ease the muscle cramps. Even with an air mattress and a sleeping bag, there was very little comfort to be found on the hard floor. Being an outdoorsman, I had readily available a veritable arsenal at my disposal. With an automatic shotgun, a deer rifle for singling out an intruder at a distance and a thirty-eight revolver strapped to my side, I was prepared to do whatever was necessary to protect my store. If the angry mobs roaming the streets of my town should decide to unleash their fury at me, I had one advantage. Because everything was dark as midnight on the inside, it gave increased visibility of silhouettes reflected in the dim light outside. Perhaps I could prevent a molotov cocktail being thrown inside and destroying everything I had worked and sacrificed to accomplish.

I desperately needed sleep, but my body was so tense I could not think of sleeping. Having camped here for many nights, I knew all of the usual nocturnal sounds. Every noise, no matter how small, that was out of the ordinary brought a quickening to my breathing and a further tension to my gut.

In order to remain awake, I forced myself to think about my past, my ancestors, my upbringing and my heritage. My thoughts wandered.

Memories came flooding back setting background music to events that sifted through my mind like a kaleidoscope.

Thinking first of my ancestors, I had to begin with Ninean Beal who was the father of the Beal family in America—

Acknowledgements

Perhaps the greatest gift of life is the essence of time. Betty Wyatt of Sky Valley, Georgia unselfishly cast aside her adversities to aid me in the development of this book. I sincerely appreciate her talents and expertise for helping to precipitate this piece of work.

Introduction

Across the years I have thought more than once about writing a book, maybe even something autobiographical. Not that my life has been all that significant. Really it has been almost commonplace, except for the fact that I, as a true southerner, was a party to one of the greatest changes that has ever swept across the South. Maybe there are those who can identify with the things I want to share.

If I had written this book the first time I thought about it, I am sure that it would have been altogether different from the way I am writing today. Not because the events that I write about were different, but because my understanding of them has changed. I see the same events, but I see them differently.

There is a word; a word called confluence that is best used when describing streams from several different places joining together and flowing as one. As I look back on my life, I recognize many times when events occurred that I did not plan. In fact, I did not even foresee them nor want them to happen. But somehow in the confluence of events, these things flowed together in ways that were sometimes rich, sometimes painful and at times I felt they were not even fair. But in the end, they have all come together and through them, my life has been changed.

THE EARLY YEARS

From Ship to Shore

As the sailing vessels made ready for Ninean Beal and his companions to leave Scotland for the New Country—America the Beautiful, the land of plenty, I can imagine how hard it was for him to say goodbye to his beloved Scotland. I can almost feel the excitement he must have felt throughout the long voyage as he anticipated the new life ahead. I haven't the slightest idea how his eyes interpreted what he saw as the ships docked in America and he made his way to what was then Georgetown.

I know that he was a very intelligent gentleman with a great appetite for land acquisition. He rapidly staked his claim to become the sole owner of thirty thousand acres. He possessed 20/20 foresight as he donated thirty acres to the United States for the construction of a new capitol. Georgetown soon changed its name to become Washington, D.C.

The majority of Ninean's land was in Maryland. This land must have been divided, sold off or otherwise disposed of. Out of all the territory with the Beal name, my brother and I inherited the deeds to twelve cemetery lots in Maryland. So far I have not even seen them.

The Beals, the Bealls and the Bells are kinfolk. Alexander Graham Bell was a direct descendent of Ninean Beal.

I don't know a lot about my ancestors. I do know there was a playboy in the crowd. His adventures have been a subject on several television documentaries. He lived in West Virginia in the late eighteen hundreds. His mama named him Thomas Jefferson Beal.

One morning Tom and a few friends set out on a hunting/gambling trip. It seems that the hunting was a front; he must have been more productive at gambling. When he returned to West Virginia, he took up residence at a friend's hotel. Tom asked his buddy to secure a metal box in his safe. He told him that he soon would be leaving on another trip and if for some reason he didn't return within a year, he could pry open the box.

Tom didn't return, but his friend waited another year before he decided it was time to check into the metal box. He discovered that the contents contained scrolls with numbers printed on them. These were ciphers that the friend could not understand. He took these papers to many people, and finally some of the scrolls were decoded and were found to contain startling information. Near a railroad track, somewhere, Tom had hidden a treasure of twenty million dollars containing gold coins and jewels. Ole Tom must have been a pretty good card shark or crapshooter to amass that kind of fortune.

The other ciphers haven't been broken. People have tried to crack them using all manner of means, even computers. Some have used books in the Bible, the Declaration of Independence and the Gettysburg Address. They were all hoping that the unbroken information would contain the exact location of the bounty.

During WWII Winston Churchill and his intellects broke the ciphers of the Germans, but nobody has solved the mystery of the rest of the numbers written on the scrolls by Thomas Jefferson Beal. The answer as to the location of the hidden treasure may have gone to the grave with him.

One clan of Beals from all over the nation has gathered once a year. They even have a newsletter printed. Every year they pack up their picks and shovels and go searching with metal detectors. They have great fun getting together, talking and planning what they will do with the treasure when they find it.

You will remember that several years ago a Mr. Fisher and his divers located ten million in gold coins out from Key West. He had his curiosity aroused by the mystery of Thomas' treasure. After doing his homework and researching all of the possibilities, one of the Fisher gang leased the property, drained an old pond that was dammed up and began excavating a farm site where they thought the treasure might be buried. While they gave it the old college try, they were unsuccessful.

Cousin Thomas didn't hide his valuables there, but I sincerely believe I have knowledge of their whereabouts. When I can find the time I, too, will be a seeker of my cousin's treasure chest. I have what I believe to be a very good hunch.

Most of the descendants of Ninean Beal traveled down the coastline following the Atlantic, settling in Virginia and the Carolinas. Some hit the trail for Texas, while others made their decision to travel north to Maine. There is a fishing village on an island out from the coast of Maine that is named Beal's Island. Most of the inhabitants are Beals.

Some of the Beals left the Carolinas to migrate south to Georgia and sunny Florida. My great-grandparents settled on the West Coast of Florida. My father's family settled in Perry, Florida, and my mother's family was from near Crystal River. James Acres Beal, Sr. chalked up four generations of his namesake. We think Acres, used as his middle name, was probably a family name passed down the line from the fact that there were so many acres of land in the early Beal family.

Lassiephine

Lassiephine Everett was the name given to a little girl born near Crystal River, Florida. The name Lassiephine has not been carried down through the family. In fact, I have never heard of anyone with the name

Lassiephine. Her mother assumed that this name made up for two. It wasn't too long before it was shortened to Lassie. I would think that she was a wee bit Scottish with a name like that.

Lassie and her sister, Etta, were actually born in a small settlement called Red Level on what was obviously a very large tract of land. In the middle of nowhere on that property was a cemetery. A dirt road leading to the graveyard was covered with beautiful moss-laden live oaks. This provided a passage and gateway to the burial grounds that was peaceful and picturesque.

Near the white folk's section, there was another fenced-in area for the graves of their slaves, and maybe a friendly Indian or two were also laid to rest there. Indian skirmishes in this part of Florida were not at all uncommon.

Lassie and Etta's homeplace would later become quite valuable property. As was all too common at that time, Lassie's mother had died while giving birth to her, and the girls were then raised mostly by their grandparents. When the grandparents died Lassie and Etta sold the property. They were paid fifty cents per acre. They were very well off for those days as they split eighteen hundred bucks.

Intuition tells me that this thirty-six hundred acres that faces on U.S. Highway 19 and runs a couple of miles to the Gulf of Mexico included many alligators and swampland. Hindsight tells me it would have been a great thing if that land had not been sold. Some fellow came along and discovered Kaolin in the front yard of the old homeplace. He purchased the mineral rights and started digging and mining. The backyard area was purchased by the Florida Power Company, where they laid out a Nuclear Plant to generate power to neighboring cities.

Like most children I loved to hear stories about my grandparents and the olden days. Mother told me that her grandfather was an officer in the Confederate Coast Guard. He had heard that the Yankees were coming and had buried his valuables somewhere behind the homeplace. He either forgot where he had hidden them or died before telling anyone of the location. When Lassie or Etta had to get up during the night to go to the potty, one would awaken the other to go out back. There really was no potty, just a two-holed privy. Might have been a stack of corn-cobs or a Sears and Roebuck catalogue between them. Many times they were frightened as they saw the orange glow of a lantern on their hill where people were digging for Grandpa's gold.

Lassie was a very smart girl and went to Tallahassee State Teacher's College to earn a degree. This college later became Florida State.

With diploma in hand she set out in her horse-drawn carriage to teach in the neighboring schools. Etta moved up to Perry where she began to take a second look at James Acres Beal. However, when she introduced him to her sister, Lassiephine, that was the end of the line for Etta. Shortly thereafter Lassie finally had three names. Their hon-eymoon was a cross-state train ride to Jacksonville Beach. She recorded some thoughts on this in her diary, dated 1923. "The hotel gave us many wonderful nights. Oceans of love and a kiss was on every wave." Beautiful!

South Georgia was different from most parts of Georgia, almost like a world of its own. A lot has changed with the yellow pines, moss-laden oaks, cypress knees, cotton fields and plantations. The cotton fields were plagued by the boll weevil, and most of the plantations were burned out or swallowed up by the Yankees. The moss-laden oaks and cypress knees are still around in abundance, and the yellow pines have become a valuable source of turpentine.

VALDOSTA

A Friendly Town

My parents decided to settle down in Valdosta, Georgia, a town just a few miles from the Florida line. This must have been a very friendly town, for in only a short while they knew just about everyone there.

The Beals were probably thought of as a cut above middle class. They both worked hard and enjoyed life very much. They were blessed with beautiful personalities and had friends from one end of town to the other. They could surely be described as a southern lady and gentleman. Not the Scarlett/Rhett type, but close. They were Christians, attending church regularly, and led their sons in the same direction.

Mama was secretary to an entrepreneur. She ran his business while he was the wheeler and dealer. He owned a boy's camp in North Carolina, an Umpire's school in Florida, and a plant farm in Georgia. His name was Mr. Carlisle, and the field hands called him Mr. Car-lite. He hopped from one state to the next. He kept no regular schedule. No one ever knew where he would be. When he died he had been in a hotel several days before anyone missed him.

Mama's office was in a tobacco warehouse across the tracks. She was responsible for shipping out plants all over the world. Colored folks did all the work to prepare them for shipping while mother directed the traffic. In one end of the warehouse was the winter quarters for a band. It was called Silus Green from New Orleans. I spent many happy hours listening to them practice. They had more rhythm than Little Richard and James Brown put together. Their rehearsals and jammin' sessions were the greatest. I looked forward each year to the return of the Silus Green Band.

Daddy

Daddy was the most conscientious, efficient executive I have ever known. He was cashier for the Atlantic Coastline Railroad. For thirty-three years he held this position and worked there until his death. He found great pleasure in his work.

As in most homes there were some nights when Mama wasn't happy. And when Mama ain't happy, ain't nobody happy. If Daddy happened to be even two cents off from balancing his report, he would not leave until he made it come out right on the penny. So we could not be sure just what time he would get home from work. I remember telling him once when I went down to see why he was so late that I would donate a nickel, then he could come out three cents ahead and come on home. But Daddy didn't work that way. He was a perfectionist. When the report balanced, then he left for home with no worries.

I was so impressed when Daddy walked out of his office to meet the train. He would strap on his pistol and carry a leather satchel out to some special car of the train. A man would slide his door open, take the satchel in and transfer the contents. Daddy would sign some sheet on a clipboard and from time to time glance over both shoulders to make sure all was well. I had a few glances of my own. (Who knew Jesse and Frank James could be around getting set for an ambush?) I had my own gun ready to help out if needed; it didn't matter to me that it was only made of wood.

I frequented the railroad yard and depot as often as I could. One of the passenger trains going through was named The South Wind. Many hours passed as I sat near the tracks, trying to catch a glimpse of the people inside, while writing stories in my mind about the travels of those I could see.

Tom Town

The Beals resided in the northern section of Valdosta. The railroad tracks dissected the business section running in a west to east direction. Most of the colored folks lived on the south side of the tracks. Families seemed to be divided by the Atlantic Coastline Railroad in many of the towns it went through. We called the colored folk's area Tom Town. I had no idea who Tom was. That was just the name for that part of town. It was that way before we arrived and would certainly be there when we were gone. To all appearances everyone seemed to be satisfied with their place in the community.

The colored folks wanted no part of the white culture, and the feeling was mutual. However, I did hear my folks make the statement quite often that "the colored people know how to enjoy a Saturday night on the other side of the tracks better than the white folks do on theirs."

They had their own schools and churches. A funeral took many days, and they seemed to bury their folk in quite a different manner from the white folk. My friends and I used to hide behind a tree and watch their baptisms at Twin Lakes—what a ceremony!

Always those being baptized were dressed in white, along with the preacher and many other church members. Everyone would gather near the water and spread out the most delicious looking array of food we had ever seen. Our salivary glands over-secreted when we saw the spread available for their consumption. Why, there was enough food to supply an army, and all my friends and I could do was watch. Oh, the fun they did seem to have. The older people would have chairs set up for them and sat fanning with paper fans from one of the funeral parlors. Being old didn't stop them from laughing, eating, and having as much fun as anyone else. There were always lots of children darting around, dressed in their nicest Sunday clothes. If any of them came too close to our hiding place, we would slide back behind a rock or tree stump until they left.

After the eatin' the food would be left out, and everyone gathered closer to the river. The preacher and the congregation praised the Lord before the dunkin', with lots of clapping and singing. As each one waded out into the water with their white gowns glistening in the rays of the sun, the preacher shouted, "Amen, Brother and Sister, Amen."

We watched what was taking place, although we couldn't understand a lot of what they were saying. We were far more impressed with the piles of fried chicken, watermelons, and mounds of cakes and pies. We were tempted to slip in and snatch some of that food, but never had the nerve to really do so. After the baptisms everyone would go back and have more to eat, and we would run back home. Our mamas never did understand why watching a baptism made us so hungry.

On their side of the tracks were Rib Shacks that sho' did smell good when the wind blew over our way. I used to hear them talk about the beer and rot gut liquor (maybe it was moonshine) that was served in the honkey tonks.

When I was a little tyke, Ish or Sam would cut my hair at the barber-shop in the hotel. They were very friendly to me. I never thought of them as a color. They were my barbers. I liked to go down to the shoeshine stands and watch the colored boy pop his rag as he slicked the polish. After I got tired of that, I would wander on downtown where some colored men sold boiled and parched peanuts, and others sang and picked their guitars. They were always laughing and seemed to be quite happy.

As I write about these events today, I cannot help but wonder if the happiness and joviality I was witness to in so many colored men and women during my childhood was just a front. If so, then they had to be the world's greatest actors.

Mint Juleps & Magnolias

My folks were very conservative. They fulfilled all the needs of their sons but were careful to weigh up the options of their pleasures. Being the younger I got spoiled just a little bit. There were times I was not too thrilled to get my brother's hand-me-downs. But most of the time I felt, ah, what the heck, it got the job done and covered up my nakedness.

I often heard the word Depression. I had no idea what that was, but I kept hearing folks talk about it. The Depression years were not what could be termed an era of mint juleps and magnolias; but Mother and Daddy managed pretty well. They built a nice three-bedroom home for brother, Jimmie, and me to call home. In fact, we were delivered there. When Mother got ripe for picking, the stork dropped in along with the doctor. Both of us were born right there at home in the guestroom. There was no need for a hospital or delivery room.

We lived in a nice, quiet residential area about three or four miles from town. Daddy was particularly proud of the yard and spent many hours supervising the work there. When I picture the old homeplace today, it is always with the azaleas and camellias in full bloom. As time progressed my folks bought another house for renting and another on Twin Lakes which was almost on the Florida line.

After I came along, Mama needed help around the house so she could go back to work. She hired a colored woman. Her name was Virginia. She was taller than average, prim and proper. She always wore a very clean, white uniform. When I started talking I could not say her name, so I called her Didi. That must have been good enough, for she answered to it for the rest of the years we knew her.

Then there was Aunt Mosouri. She looked to me like she was a hundred years old. She had big circles under her eyes, and the lower lid sagged a little.

Seeing someone who looks like Aunt Mosouri today, I would say, "She had been ridden hard and put up wet." She did not laugh much, and when she did, it seemed as if she just did so because it was expected. She didn't sound as if she really meant it. We took our dirty clothes to her. She would wash them out back in a big, black wash pot full of boiling water and lye soap. Then they would dry out on the clothesline. There was always a piece of pie or cookies laying around in her kitchen that had my name on them, and Aunt Mosouri slipped me some each time we visited.

James fit into the picture some way. His eyes were very expressive, almost protective looking. He had a very spread out Negroid type nose. James was not too tall, only about five feet eight, but he was strong as could be. He was also patient, or at least he must have been, as he taught me how to shoot marbles when he wasn't raking the yard or washing the car. I became an expert at marbles and soon had a large sack full of other boys' marbles. My favorite game was *for-keeps*.

James would often baby-sit on Saturday nights with us. I thought my folks were trying to catch up with the colored people in the having fun category because when they got home from their nights out, they sure seemed happy.

One night James had just about scrubbed the hide off our backs when he gave us a bath. When he put us to bed and tucked us in, we all heard a noise. Somebody was breaking in Mama and Daddy's bedroom. The screen had been cut and someone was opening the window. James pulled out his switchblade and slipped out on the back porch. The intruder must have seen how long James' switchblade was. It looked like Crocodile Dundee's special. Anyway, the would-be burglar began to pick 'em up and set 'em down. He jumped over our hedge, took a picket fence with him, and never paid us another visit.

James loved and protected his two little boys like we were his own. We had the same feelings. He took care of us chillun for many years. He was a dear friend and a part of our family. He later went to work for the Coca-Cola Company.

The Neighborhood Brewmeister

While Mama was carrying me, the doctor suggested that Daddy start making homebrew. This was a malt liquor full of vitamins and very nutritious he told them. Mama weighed only ninety-eight pounds and was five feet two inches tall. Daddy didn't mind this assignment at all. In fact, he became a pro and continued to make this concoction for years after I was born and his *medicine* was no longer needed. He was called The Neighborhood Brewmeister. He had so much fun with his homebrew that he later began making wine. We picked the berries, Mama made some jams and jellies and Daddy fermented what was left. We had an assembly line, siphoning, capping and placing the bottles on the shelf.

As soon as weather permitted, the Beals spent the evening in rocking chairs on the front porch, sipping a few suds. Friends in the neighborhood frequently came over to enjoy this bit of Southern Hospitality. While the grown ups sat around and visited, us chillun would go out in the yard to play *hide-and-seek* or *kick the cans*. Another activity was seeing who could capture the most lightning bugs in a glass jar. I would set my jar in the bedroom and watch them during the darkness of the night as I lay in bed. We all had a big time and hated to see the parents begin to leave and go home. We were known to try and pretend that we didn't hear them calling us and putting a close to the evening. There was a popular television show called *Evening Shade,* which reminded me of some of those happy times.

Even in my early years, I realized that Dada was very special to me. He became my buddy/friend. Every time Dada would leave for work I made sure that everyone in the neighborhood knew that I wasn't too happy. When I heard the car engine crank, I began the bawling machine. I am told I asked a thousand times a day when he was coming home and looked forward to seeing him at dinner, as we called it then. I was a daddy's boy from the word go.

When preschool time came around, Mama didn't let me sit on my little butt too much. Having been a schoolteacher, she liked to keep in practice with my brother and me. By the time I was five, I was reading and writing. She was diligent in teaching the *three R's*, as she called it— reading, 'riting and 'rithmatic.

If I wasn't doing the three R's, I was waxing furniture or washing dishes. After I overcame the fright of the vacuum cleaner, I was allowed the pleasure of pushing it around. Mama said this was all great training, but I didn't think that it was too swift.

YOUTHFUL MEMORIES

Uncle Tom's Wagon

One morning Mama told me to come with her out to the sidewalk. I had no idea what was on her mind. We stood there looking down the hill and then she said, "Here comes Uncle Tom." I couldn't see anyone, but I thought I could hear him. There was a clippity clop of the mules shodden feet and the turn of the wheels of an old slatted wagon. I could hear chanting and humming as Uncle Tom called out his list of fruits and vegetables. Soon the ladies lined up on our side of the street waiting on him.

Then he came into view. He had gray hair, was heavy set with missing teeth that showed when he smiled. He was calling out, "I got peas, ummmm. I got peanuts, okra and corn, ummah." We listened, fascinated as he had chanted the whole list. When all the purchases had been made, Uncle Tom smiled at Mama and as if she could read his mind, she said, "Sure Tom, he can go but watch out for him." Mama put me up on the back of the wagon with other kids, and we rode off laughing, talking and swinging our feet. After a few blocks, ole Uncle Tom would stop the wagon, give us grapes and peanuts and tell us to be sure and go straight back home. This became a ritual, and I was always anxious for the day when Uncle Tom came around. Thoughts of those good times are just another page to be turned in my memory book.

I was walking back home from one of these wagon rides one day when my own wheels started spinning. Aunt Mosouri must be my Aunt, but how could that be when everyone, even Mama and Daddy called her that? So Uncle Tom was not only Uncle to me but also to all my friends and family. In fact, he was the one that Tom Town was named after. There were a whole lot of Aunties and more Uncles that I got to know. We had all kind of kinfolk, but I was a little disappointed that they didn't belong just to me.

I could describe the era that I came up in as a period of neighborhood closeness, friendly get-togethers and family involvements. This certainly had to be the best time of all to land on the planet. Life was not a complexity, it was good, and it was simple. It was the good ole American way.

Playing With Fire

—Mr. Lincoln kindled the flame of discontent and was assassinated.
—Then Abolition of Slavery came about in 1863, seventy plus years before the days when Mama and I waited for Uncle Tom.
—The Sherman parade and his pyromaniac troops had scorched a trail to Savannah many years before. By my time the weeds and the trees had grown back.
—The Yankees and carpetbaggers had taken over many beautiful southern plantations.
—Soon the boll weevil ate our cotton.
—But through it all the Southern Spirit prevailed.

For three generations before mine, both sides of my family had slaves working for them. We had numerous colored people who worked for us, but by my time they were no longer called slaves and were just like family.

My mama told me, "If you play with fire, you will wet your bed tonight." I'll bet that when General Sherman and his boys spread out their bedrolls to camp out at Stone Mountain, their covers got wet.

We read about those characters in our history books when we had to. They kept on reminding us of the past. This span of time was also interrupted by WWI. The era of the thirties when I was born really wasn't a bad time to enroll in and contribute to my part of history.

The Rules of the Tavern

As I grew and left the diapers behind, I began turning into a full fledged, red-blooded American Boy. Never can I remember a time when we did not have some hired help around the home. If they had finished all their tasks, then they would start looking for something else to do. They were always there washing the car, tending to us chillun, cooking a meal, mopping or sweeping. They were a part of the family, and we grew up with them.

The Rules of the Tavern, so to speak, were never spelled out to them, only a deep understanding of what was acceptable or expected behavior was present.

—No hat on while talking to my parents.

—Always enter thru the back door.

—Sir and ma'am were required if they wanted to remain employed.

—Meals for the hired folk were eaten at the kitchen table.

—We were served in the breakfast room and the dining room.

My parents never sat down and discussed these rules with those who worked for us. It was obvious that they had been taught these things by their mamas and daddies before even asking for a job.

However, my brother and I were expected from a very early age to always be polite and remember our manners, and you can bet my parents were quick to let us know if we should forget them. My friends never failed to use the sirs and ma'ams with their hats in hand when addressing my parents, and we were expected to show the same respect for their parents, as well as our elders.

None of the colored folk who worked for us had any problems in this department that I was aware of, and no one ever had to give them a lecture. They knew that it meant food in their tummies and a roof overhead. They had to cook very little at home, as Mama always had more than enough food prepared. There would be ample leftovers to share with their families in the evening.

Catch More Flies with Honey

Once there was a colored boy who knocked politely on our back door. He said, "Scuse me Ma'am. I heard that you need somebody to work for you." He had his hat in his hand. He was black as the ace of spades, was close to seven feet tall, and weighed about a hundred and twenty-five pounds. His face was long and his eyeballs seemed to cover it up. When he smiled his teeth were white as pearls. He looked like he had ten more than he needed. Now Mama was only five feet two, and she had to lean way back to look up at his face.

She asked, "Boy, what is your name?"

He said, in a very high pitched voice, "Precious."

Looking up into the sky again, she said, "Boy, haven't you got any other name besides Precious? I don't know whether I can get used to calling you Precious. Are you sure that you don't have another name?"

"No Ma'am," he said. "Just Precious." It took Mama quite a while to quit calling him Boy and call him by his name. Precious worked for us for several years, as a handy man, working in the yard, or wherever he was needed.

I was totally unaware of any trouble communicating with the colored folks that became a part of our lives. No matter which side of the tracks we lived on we all knew that you could catch more flies with honey than you do vinegar. Each generation, colored and white, had their own set of rules, and they were just passed on down.

In present day time, our children are encouraged to think for themselves and even to question authority if they do not understand why certain things are so. But back in the days of my childhood, that just was not the case. Our parents were in charge. They told us what to do. They protected and cared for us. For the most part, we did as we were expected and simply did not ask, "Why?"

Summer Winds

When my family purchased a summer home at Twin Lakes, about twelve miles south of Valdosta, it was the beginning of many wonderful memories. I guess I look back on them as the halcyon days of my youth, because there my love for the great out of doors grew to fruition. After we packed up our things and began the drive to the lake house, it seemed as if it took forever. We did drive at a maximum speed of maybe 35 m.p.h. on the narrow highway. But, oh, the fun and excitement that we anticipated.

One bright sunny day when I was just a toddler, Mama wanted to take me down to the pier to catch a few rays. While they were splashing around and having fun, somehow I also wanted a piece of the action. I needed a change of scenery, and before they could say Jack Robinson, I was like a turtle crawling off the end of the pier. They caught me by my diaper just in time. After they had a chance to catch their breath, they decided to keep me in the water. That incident was the start of a lifelong love for the water. Only a short time thereafter I was swimming by myself. At the age of six, I swam across the lake and back, a distance of about a mile.

If there were any other activities that could be enjoyed by the Beal boys and their friends, I could not imagine them. Swimming, swinging on a rope from the trees like Tarzan, fishing, capturing snakes and diving for turtles filled our days. Mama, bless her soul, put up with everything her boys enjoyed. She never knew what would be next. If I returned home with a bucket of fish that were only big enough to have a pair of eyeballs, a backbone and a tail, she would batter and fry them.

The Turtles & the Possum

One time Daddy caught some soft-shell turtles. He prepared them for Mama to cook. She fried them to a crisp golden brown until they looked like fried chicken and served them with rice and gravy. When Mama and Daddy took a bite they declared it even tasted like chicken. Ummm good. So cautiously my brother and I tasted the turtle and went along with the chicken bit.

Sometime later Daddy brought home an opossum to fatten up. When we were called to dine on that possum one night, we watched Mama take a bite and waited for the *just like chicken*. It seemed as if it were taking a mighty long time for that one bite to get down. She chewed and chewed, and the more she chewed the bigger it got. Soon she tried to conceal the fact that it just wasn't what she expected. Even the apple in the possum's mouth didn't have any appeal. It took only a minute for us boys to let Daddy know he would be dining by himself that evening. We told him he should quit while he was ahead—the turtle, yes, but not the possum.

There were no more opossums arriving at the Beal home to garnish the supper table or be a centerpiece.

Papa

I can close my eyes and picture my granddaddy Beal. He was tall and thin, with grayish white hair and had a tendency to be cranky. Papa, as I called him, could not stand butter. So when mother baked a golden pound cake, she never let on that in addition to a dozen egg yolks she had added a whole pound of butter. I don't remember why, but Papa always wore sleeve bands, usually sported a bow tie, and enjoyed a chaw of tobacco that he cut with his pocketknife from a plug. I didn't see Papa very many times, but his visits were always special.

As a little tyke I would sit in his lap on the front porch just a rocking away. I held a bowl while Papa cut, peeled a stalk of sugar cane, and gave it to me. A lot of folks have never had the pleasure of tasting sugar cane, but I thought it was delicious. He did his best to fill up the bowl, but I was chewing and sucking out the nectar so fast I kept emptying the bowl. Come to think of it, he used the same knife to cut his tobacco and the sugar cane. I never saw him wash it either, but that didn't bother me. It didn't take away from the flavor; might even have added to it.

Papa and I had a big time together. He talked with me as if I was an adult. One day he took me fishing on the river. I can't even remember that we caught any fish, we just had a super great time being together. He taught me a lot about the woods and waters. He told me stories about when he saw Buffalo Bill in a circus. And I loved to hear him tell about his Greek friends down in Tarpon Springs, Florida. They owned restaurants and went out in the gulf to dive for sponges. The Greeks treated Papa like a king and never wanted him to leave when he went to visit. I never knew if there was a connection, but when I was older my family dined in a Greek Restaurant in Tarpon Springs called *Papas*.

Someone in Papa's generation of Beal's was a sheriff in Florida. He had an accident in which his arm was cut off at the wrist. It didn't interfere with his shooting however, as he would balance the gun on his nub.

"He could shoot the eyeball out of a rabbit," Papa told me.

None of his convicts ever tried to escape. The respect they had for him was called fear.

Papa was the only grandparent I ever knew. When I was ten my parents had to travel to Perry, Florida for his funeral. It was years before they told me Papa had committed suicide with a pistol. It was a sad ending, but good memories of him linger on.

Learnin' Is More Than Schoolin'

Shortnin' Bread

It seems all kids develop a case of mixed emotions when they begin school. My first grade teacher's name was Miss Ruth. Her first name wasn't Baby as some of us mumbled under our breath. She was so sweet, had red hair and had a whole lot of patience. She needed it with the bunch of first graders in my class.

After I became acclimated, I really enjoyed school. I remember most of my teachers through grade school and have admiration for their understanding and patience. The next nineteen years of my education brought a lot of A's and B's, and I was absent only a very few days. Mama's early teaching certainly provided a good foundation for my school years.

One very cold morning I would like to forget. I was riding my bicycle along with some friends to school. It was a three-mile ride. Some joker had swiped my handlebar grips. I didn't have gloves on and by the time we arrived at school, my little hands had frozen in the shape of the bars. When my teacher saw my frozen hands, she rushed me to the faucet and ran tepid water over them until I could stretch out my fingers and regain my circulation. I was okay but had learned a hard lesson. The next morning Mama had new grips on the bicycle, and I made sure there were gloves on my hands.

Reading, 'riting, and 'rithmatic didn't fill up all of our class time. Almost everyday we took a break to sing songs. I am sure that the fundamentals of reading music and hitting the correct notes had to be taught at some time, but it must have been on a day when I was thinking about something else. I enjoyed the singing, and still do, but I am one of those who can't carry a tune in a bucket.

The best song of all was *Mammy's Little Baby Loves Shortnin' Bread*. While I have not heard that song in years, I can remember the words as if I learned them yesterday: *"Put on de skillet, put on de lead. Mammy's little Baby gonna get some shortnin' bread."* This was our very favorite, and someone would always ask if we could sing it. The teacher had no trouble getting us to open up and sing with gusto. This was a happy tune!

Other songs we learned to enjoy were *Camptown Races (Do Da, Do Da)*, *Old Black Joe* and *Old Folks At Home*. We enjoyed any of the songs that were written by Stephen Foster. We either learned them at school, or my folks taught us to sing them while traveling in the car. Believe me, whenever we went on a trip there seemed to be lots of time for singing. It was hard for me to sit still for very long, and even today I don't care to spend too much of my time cooped up in a car.

Another favorite of mine was *Ole Man River*. I think it was best sung by a colored man named Paul Robeson. It depicted a scene on a dock on the Mississippi River. The song brings to mind steamboats and colored folks working, probably loading cotton bales. It must have been about a Saturday because of the words, *"you get a little drunk and land in jail, but ole man river just keep on rollin' along."*

My folks used to love to hear Al Jolsen sing *Mammy* and *Old Folks At Home*. Those songs were wonderful entertainment on the radio as we sat on the front porch in the evening.

Sandbar Romance

One of my closest boyhood friends was named Billy. He lived just around the corner from me. Billy was a year younger than I and had a sweet tooth that could never be filled. One time he had been looking over the shoulder at someone hammering a nail into a board. He was standing too close. The hammer came back and broke off a part of Billy's two front teeth. This left him with the appearance of having teeth angled like a beaver.

He and I had a night time signal to attract each other's attention. We thought nobody else could hear our whippoorwill whistle. No one else ever paid any attention to it anyway. Through the years we camped out many nights with our dogs.

One time Billy and I were camped out on the Withlacoochee River. We were having more than our share of fun. We set up our tent, nibbled on something and set out bank hooks on the river. After swimming for a while, we fished some more. We heard happy voices down where the river made a turn to create a sandbar. We crawled on our tummies like Indians 'til we could see over the cliff what was happening.

There we found several colored folks swimming in shorts, panties and bras. We noticed they had a watermelon on the sandbar. They were having a big ole time like it was 'cross the tracks on a Saturday night. They would swim for a while and return to the sandbar to the watermelon. As we looked closer we noticed they were not eating that 'melon like we were used to. There were a bunch of holes cut in the topside with straws sticking out. They sucked on those straws, talked and laughed for a while, and went out swimming again. Soon they were laughing and carrying on like they were all on a high, swigging the nectar concoction. They must have all decided to leave at the same time, and they even forgot to put on the rest of their clothes. They just went out into the woods by couples and went in separate directions. We were sorry to see them leave. When I got a little older, I decided they hadn't left at all.

Billy wanted to go down and see if there was any watermelon left, but as it looked like their fun was all over we made our way back to camp. Billy's dad later told us they must have had *shine* poured down in the melon.

Every once in a while Billy's dad would get a wild hair and take us to Otter Creek, a few miles south of Valdosta. He had once sung with the Florida Minstrels and often would sing or hum tunes as we rode down. I can hear him now as he sang *He's a Traveling Man, Ain't Nothing but a Traveling Man* in his deep bass voice. He taught us how to play a tune on a saw with the eraser end of a pencil. I didn't think we could carry a tune in a bucket, but when he said we were good that's all we needed to hear. I am sure that I remember being the one to catch most of the fish, and we would take them home to Billy's mama. She really knew how to cook them.

Boom!

It seems that I was always getting into some kind of trouble. One Christmas I got a bangsite cannon. I was so proud of it. The directions said, press the valve, let the fluid run into the powder and the gas would evolve. Then push the plunger to make a spark. It really shot like a cannon and was supposed to be perfectly safe and wouldn't even set tissue paper on fire.

One day my friend, Pat, and I were playing in a hut we had constructed from dog fennel and broom straw. We were playing with this *safe* cannon. Boom! Boom!…and the field in the middle of the neighborhood was on fire. It was late that afternoon before Pat and I showed up at home—after all the fire trucks had gone. Mama had always said that I should never play with fire, or I would sho nuf wet the bed. I don't remember if I wet the bed that night, but I'm sure that I came close to it after the scolding I received. Needless to say, that was the end of my bangsite cannon.

Here Come De Judge

There was a Judge who lived in Valdosta who later became President of the American Turpentine Farmer's Association. Over the years he had purchased more than 150,000 acres of pine forests in southern Georgia, near the Florida line and had access to possibly another 150,000 acres. Back then he could buy this land for fifty cents to a dollar an acre. If my dad and some of his friends saw Judge Langdale coming down the sidewalk towards them, they would swiftly cross to the other side of the street. They knew that he would hit them up for a loan of fifty cents or so towards the purchase of these yellow pine woods. He knew that this land would in time be quite valuable. Most of this land was between Valdosta and Waycross. One time the Judge was written up in the *Saturday Evening Post* as owning more land than anyone in the United States.

From time to time he would invite some of his friends to come spend a few days hunting at an area he had on this land out in the Okefenokee Swamp, very near the Florida border. Most of his guests were doctors and lawyers. One time he invited a friend of mine, Conrad Williams, to come down for a week and told him he could bring a friend. Conrad's father was a doctor, and Judge Langdale was a friend of his family. Conrad also became a doctor and is now practicing in Valdosta, Georgia. Being as I have always loved the out-of-doors, those days will rank high on my list of special events. There was a shanty built for sleeping, one of those where you threw your sleeping bag on a slatted floor, and listened to the wind blowing through the holes between the boards that made up the sides of the shanty. At least there was a type of roof overhead that provided some protection from the rain.

There was another shanty like this for eating, with two or three black men who did all the cooking and cleaning. Now the nighttime activity was playing poker. Most of the people who came to this camp were very wealthy, but you could have heard their voices raised in protest for miles around if they were dealt a losing hand. The stakes were never very high, but anyone listening to the protests would have thought they were about to lose everything they owned.

We had plenty of good food and lots of beverages to drink. I don't believe I will ever forget getting up to go and visit with Mother Nature when I heard the Judge call out for me to not stop at one particular tree. He told me go about ten feet further across the creek, and then I would be in Florida and it would be alright to go there.

When we finally went to bed and got snuggled down in our sleeping bags, we listened to the multitude of noises and sounds coming through the night from the swamp. There was a pot-bellied stove that sat out in the middle of the shanty floor, and we lay in a circle around the stove. The black men who did the cooking kept the fires banked only until about midnight, and it could get quite cold before morning. Before daylight came we would be awakened to the smell of coffee being brewed. We were brought some in a metal cup. I remember wrapping both hands around that cup, which was so hot I could hardly hold on to it. However, the warmth in my hands was almost as welcome as the warmth that coffee gave my system.

Breakfast at that camp was a feast fit for a king. The Judge told us every morning to be sure and eat a lot because the truck would not be by to pick us up until supper-time. After breakfast we piled into an old beat up truck with our shotguns, while the Judge got on his white horse with shotgun by his side. Along with his dogs he rode out through the swamps and would run deer back toward us. The truck driver would let one of us off every one hundred yards or so, and we would sit on a stump and wait for the deer. The driver would pick the place for us to wait, and he would say, "He came right by here last year!"

When we made it back to camp in the late evening, the smells of supper coming from the cooking area were rivaled only by the taste of another wonderful meal. These were great times, and I enjoyed this way of deer hunting. Quite a difference from most of my hunting trips.

Saving Lives

The YMCA was a super organization for us to enjoy. We met at the Georgia State College for Women, which changed its name to Valdosta State sometime in the 1950's.

The counselors taught us archery, tennis, golf and swimming. While I loved tennis and later played on the tennis team during college, I must have majored in swimming and diving. I really excelled in those sports. I never won less than a blue ribbon. Well, maybe I don't want to remember getting any others, but I know I was good. My training there helped me to later get a job at the Valdosta Country Club as a lifeguard. I had an instructor at the Y named Noah Langdale. He was built like a bull. Noah would grab me by one leg and throw me to the other end of the pool. He was an All-American Tackle and later became the President of what is now Georgia State University in Atlanta.

Because of my lifeguard training, I rescued many swimmers in distress and saved a great number of lives. One summer day I was enjoying soaking up a few rays on a raft at Twin Lakes. The raft was tied to the pier that extended to a tower. The pavilion was bursting at the seams with the Sunday afternoon crowd. The tower was for diving and stood in about twenty feet of water. People began screaming and pointing toward the tower. That got my attention and I turned just in time to watch a young man going down for his last chance. About thirty seconds later, I was following him to the bottom. My timing was perfect. I got him to the top and moved him toward the shore with a cross-chest carry.

When I made it to where I could stand up in the water, I was trying to get him to the pier when a friend of mine waded out to help. This young man was very big, and it took both of us to pick him up at dead weight. When I got him into a prone position, it took very little artificial respiration to save him. When he got his color back and I knew that he was alright, I slipped away from the crowd. I had no idea that my friend remained and took all the glory. When the young man's parents arrived, they just couldn't thank my friend enough.

The next day, the *Daily Times* printed the story along with a picture of my friend. The local merchants were so proud of their hero that they gave him a two-year scholarship to the university of his choice, along with a five hundred dollar merchants' gift certificate. To my knowledge my friend never used the scholarship after I confronted him with the situation and reminded him that he was acting under false pretense. It crushed my feelings a little bit, and I certainly could have used the scholarship.

While I was at my peak of swimming, I had an opportunity to visit my cousins at Miami Beach. We were enjoying the facilities at the McFaden Deauville Hotel. While I was assuming the horizontal, with a few layers of Coppertone, my cousin yelled, "Look at the old couple caught by the undertow."

I took off as fast as I could. I either had no fear or no brains. When I swam past the old man, heading first for the woman, he called out to me, "No, no. Don't save her. Save me!"

I will never forget that little fat man yelling those words to me in his high pitched voice. I ignored him, swam out to save his wife and then returned for him. I got them both safely on the beach, gagging and trying to get back their breath. The crowd gathered around, and soon the lifeguard arrived. For some reason I avoided the crowds and conversation. I felt only disgust for the old man and wanted no words from him. I had my own sense of satisfaction through saving their lives.

R-E-S-P-E-C-T

My Best Friend

There were very few things that seemed to irritate my dad. He possessed only a couple of idiosyncrasies that I can recall. One thing that really got his dander up was anyone coming into his office smacking his or her lips on a wad of gum. He would immediately stop in the middle of whatever he was doing and say, "When you get through smacking your gum, I'll be happy to wait on you."

It made no difference to him who it was. He figured respect warrants respect and was very sincere about this. I used sir and ma'am when addressing my parents as long as my mama and daddy lived. It didn't denote servitude at all. It was as Aretha Franklin sang it, *R-E-S-P-E-C-T*. This gesture also showed my appreciation for the accumulation of sacrifices they had made for me. It was a form of love and thanks for the provisions of my future and a roof over my head.

Like the remembering to say our sirs and ma'ams, there was another ironclad rule that Daddy laid in the groundwork of my memory. He told me that if someone called me a son of a bitch, I was to remember that person was not cursing me, but my mother. He also said that if I didn't make that person take it back, either by words or force, then if he found out about it, he would give to me what I should have given to the person who called me that. Daddy was not even close to being mean, but he did command respect. He never had to punish us for that one. We got his message loud and clear.

Woods & Water

My dad was an excellent and very skilled outdoorsman. His cohorts gave him all the room he wanted as a sportsman. Fishing or hunting, he was Grade A-Prime. Seldom, if ever, can I recall his returning home without a vest full of birds or a string of fish.

He loved the challenge of the outdoors and developed his own techniques for thrashing the water that the fish seemed to love. His fellow sportsmen said they would definitely not follow him on a lake, because he left them very few finny critters to catch. He also crafted his own jon boats. Whatever my Dad enjoyed, I assumed that I would join him. Sometime his method of sharing the fun was not quite what I expected. In my earlier years he had one motor for his boat, and it was only powered by one horse—me! I was the horse with a paddle, but I loved it.

He enjoyed following his pointers through the fields and pinewoods in search of Bob White Quail. He related to me that training his dogs and finally witnessing a point was like the epitome of hand tying a fly and enticing a trout with it.

The first time Dad got up the courage for his boys to tag along on a hunting trip was a fiasco. I am sure it was a humiliating experience for him. We were too young to hunt and were just going along to watch. He was so proud of his dogs completing their training and wanted us to see what that training was all about. As we tried to keep up with him, it took two of our steps for each one of his. He had been walking a couple of hours with such excitement and success that he forgot about his chillun. When he did stop to look over his shoulder, his boys were both so pooped out they were taking a nap under a shade tree. At times the dogs even entertained the same idea. We told Dad that he should have been a postman; we were sure the mail would never have been delivered so quickly. I don't think he took us to WATCH his dogs many more times.

When he first started taking me on his hunting trips, I dressed the part of the mighty hunter, boots and all. But as he shot the birds, I had the privilege of fetching them to him.

Throughout the years I have reflected on the variances between his abilities and mine. He was a top-of-the-line sportsman, and I considered myself a close second to him. Without really acknowledging the fact, I tried very hard to be as good as he at anything we did.

Dad worked hard to purchase a case of shells and with a couple of boxes packed in his hunting vest, his expectations were higher than I could even imagine. He was not too happy if he didn't bring down twenty or more birds with the twenty-five shells in a box. Every shot counted with Daddy. If I hit ten birds out of a box and frightened the other fifteen, I considered myself to be an expert. I always said I was keeping the others flying so the next guy could have a shot.

The difference in our approach was that the family would be depending on what he returned home with for a meal. His was out of necessity. It was food for supper that evening, while mine was for fun. Mine would add to the amount on the table, but I did not feel the pressure he must have felt.

There were no such things as gourmet foods in Mama's kitchen. However, I thought she was the greatest cook ever. We had some freezer paper to wrap fish and fowl, but they did not stay in the freezer long before they were needed. There were no freezer bags available for long-term storage.

Most of the time my family would be dining that evening on the catch or kill of the day. It normally was from field or stream to the platter. Now when I get the opportunity to fish, I always filet our catch of the day and place it in a *Ziploc* freezer bag full of water. Things will keep that way for maybe a year.

One of the meals I enjoyed most was when Mama prepared a dish she termed as Perleau. It couldn't have had any calories, for only a pound of pure butter was used to slowly simmer the birds. She would cook them until the meat just fell off the bones and then place it on a bed of rice for serving. Just writing about it makes my mouth water.

Perleau, I was told, was a French word. Other terms used around home I assume were French also; Port o cachet—for carport and Daveneau—for sofa. I am most likely sure that the spelling is not correct, but I was also raised on phonics, and if pronounced the way I have spelled them, that should be close enough.

I never knew why or where those words came from, but they were a part of our every day vocabulary, just like saying sir and ma'am.

Remembering the Razor Strap

I can remember only one spanking that Daddy gave me. I'm not saying that I didn't deserve to have more. One day Jimmie and I were playing chase all over the house. Mama had been telling us to get dressed and go play outside. Daddy had worked hard since early that morning, removing old linoleum from the bathroom floor and replacing it with new. Mother came in to pass inspection, and they were very pleased over a job well done. They walked outside to get a breath of fresh air.

Meanwhile the game of chase was gaining momentum. I ran into the bathroom and slammed the door. Jimmie forced his way in, and I let the door fly. It caught just enough linoleum to peel it back. When **The Man** came in to see why we were so quiet, he saw his day's work ruined.

He picked up his razor strap and asked, "Who's first?"

He began peeling the hide off our little butts. That was the first and last time that I recall getting a spanking from him. It only took one time for me to realize that was just about all of that kind of fun my skinny little behind could take for a lifetime. Back in those days, I never heard the terms child abuse or cruelty to children. We deserved what was given, and we learned our lesson.

Like most older brothers, Jimmie was very thoughtful and kind. When we had homemade ice cream, which was frequently, he would sit on top of the churn and keep it steady while allowing me the privilege of turning the handle. When the ice cream would begin to get hard and the turning became slower and slower, he would encourage me by talking about how good it would be and urge me to turn that handle faster. Jimmie allowed me that kindness for many years before I caught on.

Crawl 'Fore You Walk

Daddy had his own philosophy about, "We should all crawl 'fore we walk." I inherited the same attitude, I am sure, from him.

The very first piece of hunting equipment that I was handed was a homemade slingshot. I watched as Dad found a good forked stick that would fit the palm of my hand. Then he cut two pieces of rubber innertube and attached them to the fork. After tying a string from each end of the rubber to the holes cut into a shoe tongue, he gave it to me and said, "The rest is up to the hunter."

I even got to sit under a tree and flail away at the birds that perched in it. I may not have hit any of them, but I surely scared the devil out of them.

When Dad thought it was time, I was given a Daisy Air Rifle. I got to be a champ with that. One morning I had been on one of my safaris through the neighborhood. I was returning home with a Yellow Hammer, which is a variation of the woodpecker family. An ole colored woman stuck her head out the back door as I was walking through a backyard.

She said, "Boy, what choo gonna do wid dat bird?"

I told her I was going home to give it to my cat.

She said, "Boy, please let me have dat bird."

I asked what she was going to do with it. She replied that she would batter, fry it, and have it for dinner.

So I gave her the bird and she said, "Boy, you don't know how much I appreciate dis bird. But, whatever you do don't bring me no mockin bird."

I asked her why.

With a hearty laugh she told me, "Cause a mockin bird tells all he knows, and if you eat one you will tell all you know."

Since that day I have never eaten a mockingbird, and I guess that I never will.

I progressed in my hunting, leaving the air rifle to a single barrel shotgun and single shot rifle. Later, much later, I had a double barrel and an automatic. I also grew out of being the only one-horse engine in the boat, for occasionally Dad would take over for a while. But I was always aware of who was the captain of our ship.

My Dad was a very handsome gentleman and respected by everyone. He was encouraged throughout the years to run for Mayor of Valdosta. He always refused, telling them, "I love my friends and wish not to make an enemy."

He took great pride when he got all dressed in his Masonic apron or Shriner's outfit. I would sit and watch as he put each piece on. I imagined he was wearing an admiral's coat, then his pirate's hat. The outfit would be complete when he slipped on his Confederate sword. This little tyke's mind sure did wander, my imagination ran wild as I watched him prepare to slay any dragons he might meet.

Mother worshiped the ground he walked on, and we could tell the feelings were mutual. All of their love and compassion seemed to spill over to their two sons. We were very fortunate.

When I was ten or eleven I went with my folks all the way down to Key West. I could not believe the seven-mile bridge. Back then it was wooden. The views were gorgeous, but I did not feel very secure while we were on the bridge. My daddy drove even more slowly than usual so he and Mama could admire the scenery. I just wanted him to speed up a little bit and make it to the other end. At that tender age even Mr. Hemingway's house and the southernmost point of Florida didn't grab me. My interests were more toward the fish I saw brought in by the boats at the Marina. I noticed some boys about my size that sorta looked like me. Papa used to say my hair was as black as two crows and often called me the Brown Bomber. I assumed this was after Joe Lewis, since I was always so tanned. These boys had the same color hair, and I was just about as tan as they were. When people tossed coins in the water, they would dive in and retrieve them. Daddy had to grab me to prevent my joining them. These boys were nicknamed Conchs. Mama took my picture with them, and we looked like brothers.

With the 20/20 hindsight that I possess, I am aware now that Mama sacrificed many times to let me take her place with her mate. When Dad and I would plan a float trip on the river for early the next morning, Mama would be the one to watch us drift lazily down the rapids telling us to have fun. I was very proud when the day arrived for me to be able to reciprocate, wave them goodbye, and know that they could spend a beautiful day together.

God Don't Love Ugly!

My parents never minded all the kids in the neighborhood coming to my home to play. We tore up the shrubbery and wore out patches of grass, but our friends were always welcome.

When there was a large group gathered, we often went to the lawn of Georgia State Women's College that was nearby. This later became Valdosta State. When I was twelve I remember a colored boy who walked across town to watch us playing ball there. Sonny watched for awhile, and soon I asked if he would like to play with us. He turned out to be a very good athlete. When the game was over, we went our way and Sonny went his. We never gave it a thought, it was just our way of life. We were having fun and growing up.

One morning several of my friends and I went duck hunting. On our way back home one of the guys said, "Let's have some fun and drive thru Tom Town."

Their idea of having a good time was quite different from mine. They sighted in on a colored woman who was walking down the dirt road with a basket full of clothes balanced on her head. The boy driving the car went close to her, took a paddle, and stuck it out of the window. When he popped her on the rear, it scared her more than it hurt. It made her drop the basket of clean clothes. Just as it happened the car choked down and along with the woman's squeals, the neighbors came out on their front porches to see about the commotion. All of us in the car, except the driver, jumped out and pushed it faster than it could run under normal conditions. I was not too proud to be a part of that little escapade.

Like Mama always told me, "God don't love ugly." I knew that what had been done that day was ugly. Needless to say that was the last time my friend drove his car through Tom Town.

When I was growing up we often swam at Barber's pool. He had concreted up the sides of a natural pool, built a diving board, and for ten cents we could go swimming. The pool was fed by spring water and was cold as the devil. Rules were strictly enforced. No horsing around, no glass containers, boys were to wear an undershirt, and girls a bathing cap.

Can you imagine what Mr. Barber would say if he got a look at the bathing attire of today? Just one view of the cleavage bulging, crotch-hugging bikinis would be more than enough to permanently close down his pool. In the recent Olympics in Atlanta, one of the female participants in track and field actually ran in an outfit designed for complete freedom and showing of the buttocks. I was amused when I saw the suits that the men from the United States might be wearing in this year's Olympics. They are made of spandex and consist of a top and bottom. Now, if Mr. Barber were around, he would certainly approve, because most of the suits worn by the boys around his pool were two pieced and made of wool!

There was, and remains, an everlasting joke in our family. Papa would ask, "What is blacker than a crow?"

Of course, the answer was, "A couple of crows," and my bushy head of black hair was always compared to that. Mama used to tell me that I had seven cowlicks, and that my hair ran "Forty ways for Christmas." It was just about impossible to keep it combed down. So, at an early age, Mama parted my hair in the middle, brushed it straight back and I slept with one of her old stockin's on my head. Even this didn't provide much help, and I often looked a lot like Alfalfa on the *Little Rascals*.

Both Mama and Daddy also had coal black hair, but my brother Jimmie's hair was so blond it was almost white. When he swam in a pool that had an over-abundance of chlorine, the sun even bleached it more and turned it a sickly shade of green. People were constantly asking him where he came from, and who was his daddy.

Daddy jokingly told Mama that the Fuller Brush Man must have stayed too long one day. He was the only one who came around with blond hair. I still remind my brother that we couldn't have had the same daddy. There must have been a blonde in the wood pile.

Country Club Life

Since Daddy enjoyed so many outdoor sports he saw no reason to join the Valdosta Country Club. He had a lot of friends who were members and played golf, but golf was definitely not his cup of tea. Golf was, and still is to some extent, considered by some to be a rich man's game.

When I was working at the Valdosta Country Club, I had many colored friends. I remember Lester who was one of the greenskeepers, and Lawson who worked in the pro shop. The caddies and I often played tonk (a card game) in the barn. We didn't care about color, except the green color of money. We didn't have to integrate to enjoy each other; we were friends, and it was natural. I didn't have colored friends at school or at church, because there were none there for me to associate with.

When I began working as a lifeguard there, teaching swimming during the day and tennis at night, I had the opportunity to watch the golfers on the greens. I watched their approach shots and noted how they putted. It took only a short time for me to catch the fever. I bought a second hand set of clubs. When almost everyone had finished their rounds, I could slip out with some of the colored caddies and play a few holes.

I thought I had learned a good bit about the game by spending so much time watching. My very first shot landed (due to a slice, of course) two fairways over from the one I was supposed to be playing. There was a foursome there getting ready to hit their next shots on that very same fairway where my ball was headed. One big ole bruiser reached down to pick up his ball, and either his or my timing was perfect. When he raised up and located the one who had hit him on the rear with that ball, he looked like a Brahman Bull charging across the pasture. I didn't know whether to run and give up the game forever or what! I was familiar with the saying, "God doesn't love a coward," but this time I had second thoughts. But, I remained to face the music. The Goliath had cooled off by the time he got to me, or he might have noticed the look of terror on my face and my shaking legs. Anyway, he handed my ball back and said, "Be more careful, son."

That was one time when I emphatically said, "Yes Sir." Since that day I have been just a little more careful. I learned my lesson quickly.

In addition to lifeguarding and teaching swimming and tennis at the Country Club, I also taught both sports to the officers' wives and children at Moody Air Force Base. Over a period of six or seven years, I calculate that I taught a couple of thousand women and children how to swim. This enabled me to save up enough funds for four or five years of college.

One year I was written up as being the Pied Piper of the Valdosta Country Club. I loved the children, and they seemed to enjoy my attention and playing with them. I really was happy during those days at the Country Club. Lifeguarding, teaching swimming and tennis were really the only way I could see what the Country Club life was all about.

The Gentle Winds

My folks made sure that decency, courtesy and respect for others were a part of our everyday living. When I joined the Boy Scouts of America, they contributed further to what my parents had instilled. Each meeting the Scout Oath was repeated in unison. Being reverent and courteous were the main ingredients along with thrifty, brave and clean. Once in a while though, we did manage to get a little dirty.

My parents took my brother and me to Sunday school and church when we were infants, and worship and fellowship have always been a part of my life. Even the Scout meetings were held at the church. When I became a Tenderfoot, I was also the Troop Scribe. I have been writing from that day on. Earning merit badges was a goal I worked hard for, and when I attained the rank of Eagle Scout, I was just as proud of that accomplishment as my parents. Being involved in Scouting was an excellent way to travel through my boyhood days. It did a lot for my gray matter during puberty also.

Our code for living included manners, respect and Sunday school. The Golden Rule bit was a must. Love all men without hatred, a good education and religion were a part of our everyday life—we weren't to be just Sunday Christians. Watch your language and be in by nine. We had breakfast, dinner and supper, and we all ate together. I sho didn't want to be late, as Mama's cookin' was the best. We had no television. Sometimes we listened to the radio or read a funny book. Never was race discussed. On Saturday morning we occasionally got to go to a Cowboy movie if all our chores were done. As I look back it seems as if the winds of time blew gently during those days. If there was ever very much for me to be unhappy about, I didn't know it.

Crossing the Line

Memory's eye brings another lasting impression formed while I was learning about the world. When we traveled south to Twin Lakes, many times I would see convicts working on the side of the roads. While most of them were black, there were some white men there too. They all wore striped, white and black outfits. Some, I assumed were very bad, because they wore a ball and chain. When they were moved from place to place, they were herded like animals into a cage on wheels. Sometimes they would look up as we passed, and I would get a very eerie feeling and was happy to get on by them. All of the guards were white men, wearing pistols and carrying shot guns. From time to time we would hear about someone who had escaped, and I wondered if their guards had found it necessary to use those guns.

I have never shared another memory that I have with anyone. My friend and I would go by every once in a while to see another friend and his sister. We were all around ten at the time. This particular day we dropped in for a visit after school. The brother had a butcher knife, and he was very upset over the fact that the colored boy who worked there had just attacked his sister. The boy was probably eighteen. It really frightened us, and we left immediately.

I had heard stories about things that were supposed to have happened when a colored boy messed around with a white girl. If these stories were true, had we gone home and told our parents, then that colored boy would have most likely been strung up and lynched. This was the era when there was a point at which you simply did not cross the race boundary. It was never talked about, you just didn't do it. Something like this was unheard of at that time in my town.

I have kept this in my craw for all of these years. My friend and I never spoke of this incident again. I don't know what, if anything, happened when we left their house, and I never asked.

Equality

One evening Dad and I were sitting in the car waiting for Mama to finish her day at the office. I saw a woman walking across the tracks carrying a basket of clothes on her head and said to Daddy, "Look at that colored lady. Doesn't she look funny?"

I discovered what the saying, "Silence cuts deeper than the sharpest sword," really means. This wound was getting deep, and somehow I knew that his silence was not golden. The moment of his silence seemed like an eternity. I knew that I had just placed both feet in the proverbial bucket. I was not really sure why, but I had stepped right in the middle of it. If I could have crawled through the back seat, I know that I would have tried.

Finally, after Daddy came to his senses and regained his thoughts, I heard these words, "Do you consider that woman to be equal to your Mother?"

"No Sir," I quickly said, knowing that was the answer he wanted.

He then informed me that he had best never, ever let him hear me call a colored woman a lady again. "She is a woman, not a lady." He made sure I heard this. Right or wrong, this is the way my daddy was brought up, and he wanted to make damned good and sure that I also was programmed this way. His father and those before him were cut from the same pattern. As with the wind, time changes, and I consider myself fortunate to be living in a time where the term *lady* is determined by one's character instead of the color of their skin.

Both my parents were born at the turn of the century. Only a couple of generations ahead of them, their folks had owned slaves. While many families still had slaves during my parents' time, there was one difference. They did not own them, they were not bonded anymore, and were free to come and go as they pleased. Many chose to stay right there on the farms or land belonging to their bosses. Some began moving to areas like Tom Town where they could live close to other blacks. I cannot remember when we did not have blacks working around the house. The term slaves was not used. We called them servants or help. This was and is not racial hatred, just different cultures and avenues of life.

I have never been afraid of work. I would say that I could curl up right by it and go to sleep. But I honestly cannot remember when I didn't work. My first two years of high school I had a paper route delivering *The Valdosta Times*. Rain, snow, sleet or shine I pedaled my bike four miles to town to pick up my papers and delivered them on the way back. The route began about three miles from home and finished a couple of blocks past it. There were one hundred and fifty-six customers on that route, most of who were kind to me. I can't say the same for some of their dogs. Their bill was $1.80 per month, and if I were lucky I would get a 20-cent tip. Boy, howdy, it did make me humble. There were many mornings when I would have preferred to roll over and stay in that warm bed, but having been taught *sticktoittiveness,* that was never an option. Somehow Mama taught me to save and after a couple of years, I had enough in savings to send me through another year of college.

During my nineteen years of schooling, there were no colored boys and girls in any of my schools. I never wondered why. They had their own schools and colleges just like we did. I remember Albany State, Fort Valley and Morris Brown Colleges were for the colored people.

I was never in a social or fraternal club where there were coloreds. There were none in the churches either. This separatism was taken for granted, and I never gave it a thought. Why should I? Everybody seemed to be happy. The way we were brought up served like a traffic light for my generation. We didn't question our parents' ways. We knew we were loved, and it never even occurred to us to ask why.

Tragedy

One morning Daddy was out in the yard supervising a well company driving down a pipe. He wanted to have an artesian well to be used for watering purposes. We were in the midst of a drought that summer and needed more water. Daddy took great pride in his yard and gardening. Hundreds of azaleas and camellias really made our home a showplace. There were two colored men driving the pipe down with sledgehammers. Daddy was nice enough to hold the pipe for them, when somehow his fingers were in the wrong place at the right time. He had to be rushed to the hospital for amputation of the tips of three fingers.

At this time I was a senior getting ready to graduate from the Southern College of Pharmacy in Atlanta. This later became the Mercer Southern College of Pharmacy. I received a letter from Daddy telling me about the accident. That weekend Mama called me to say that Daddy wasn't doing too well. The doctor had been out and given him a shot to make him rest.

While driving home to see the best friend that I ever had, my thoughts were about how he had played such an important role in my twenty-five years. I obviously listened to every word that he said.

When I arrived, Mama greeted me and said Dad was in the guestroom asleep. I sat at the foot of his bed assuming that if anything were serious he would have been in the hospital. The doctor had injected a shot of morphine to relieve the pain in his arm and chest.

He also was taking Donnatal to relax his stomach. Mama was busy in the kitchen, when suddenly I saw my old friend and companion gasping for his last breath. Back in those days we had only artificial respiration, no mouth-to-mouth resuscitation. I did what I could while Mama called the doctor.

When he arrived, he said, "I'll try pressure on his chest, but I'm afraid he is gone."

What happened to Dad when he had the accident was evidently a sloughing off of a clot in his blood stream and a shock to his system.

There were several hundred friends at the funeral, among them many colored folks who came by to pay their respects. While traveling to Sunset Hills in the procession, my Uncle Don told me to turn around and look at all Daddy's friends in their cars behind.

He said, "When I die, I'll be lucky to have the neighbors on each side of me come to pay me respect."

He was absolutely right. There were no neighbors at his funeral, just family. Uncle Don had outlived all of his friends.

Many times I was told that the reason the Beals never left Valdosta was due to the many friends they had. They loved their friends and neighbors.

For three days I was in such a state of shock, that I could not shed a tear. Finally, late the fourth evening I stood in the yard outside our home looking down at the well pipe and Daddy's beautiful flowers. My life with him was turning another page. I then realized that he was gone, and the tears came coursing down my cheeks.

Mama lived on for quite a few more years. Daddy was only fifty-two when he died. Mama seldom showed her grief to me. She was a little lady but was very strong and had a lot of spunk. The example of her love for her mate was passed on to her chillun and friends. She kept on keeping on.

One day she asked how I would feel if she began seeing a very nice gentleman. This was many years after Dad's death.

I said, "Whatever makes you happy."

The new acquaintance was good for Mama. He was very industrious, owned about a thousand acres of farmland and lived by himself on that farm. They went to movies and out to supper with more and more frequency. I could tell they were beginning to become serious, and one day Mama asked what I thought about them making a life together.

But that was not to be. Before very long tragedy struck her life again. This man paid his workers at the same time each week. One of his field hands that knew about when he would have his cash at home murdered his boss and stole the cash. This was a devastating blow to Mama.

Fortunately my Uncle Don and Mama's sister, Etta, did a lot of traveling all over the United States. Mama would tag along with them many times. They owned a home up in the mid North Georgia mountains, and Mama had gone up for a visit with them. This trip turned out to be her last earthly journey.

On a Sunday afternoon I opened my pharmacy after church. I was busy filling prescriptions when a phone call interrupted everything. It was my Uncle Don calling to tell me that Mama was with them and seemed to be having a problem—some kind of congestion in her chest. What should he do?

The next thing I heard was, "I believe she is dying! In fact, she is. What can I do?"

After explaining how to give mouth-to-mouth and anything else I could think of to help for about ten eternal minutes, he told me that my mama had passed away. By then there was a crowd in my pharmacy sharing my sadness. Mama had died with congestive heart failure. Not only was she my dear mama, she was also a dear friend whom I loved throughout the wonderful years we shared.

I am the only guy I know who tried to save both of his parents. It's tough to write so personally about my grief in the pages of a book and relate the death of my loving friends. They were such an integral and important part of my life, though, that my strong love for both of them cannot be overlooked and will always remain with me. They gave me a beautiful and happy childhood and encouraged me in my profession. I have wonderful memories of both of them.

THE SCHOOL OF HARD KNOCKS

Timing Is Everything

I recall quite vividly Christmas Eve, 1940. I could hardly contain my excitement as I tried to sleep. I had asked for a chemistry set and was thinking of all the experiments that I wanted to try. I could just picture that set under the Christmas tree and sure enough, on Christmas morning, there was a Gilbert Chemistry Set. My mama and daddy had no idea of the number of hours I would spend absorbed in my experiments, lost in my own little world. They also could not have known that little chemistry set was definitely an instrument that would lead me into my future.

I leaned toward science throughout my education and soon knew that I wanted to be a part of the medical profession. I had visions of becoming a pediatrician or an orthodontist. During my undergraduate years, I mailed literally dozens of applications to various colleges all over the nation. The first year I sent ten or twelve applications. I labored over getting together all of the information each school required. My work at the Valdosta Country Club as a lifeguard paid thirty-five dollars a week. That was exactly the amount of the fee that had to be enclosed with each application. As I dropped these into the mailbox, I felt a sense of relief, excitement, and anticipation. I watched our mailbox everyday for replies to come in, feeling that I would surely be accepted at one or more schools. The first reply came back negative, so did the second, as did every application I had made. Everyone was telling me not to let it get me down, just try again next year. I knew that my grades certainly weren't the problem, so that is just what I did. I sent out more applications, some to the same schools the next year, and the next and the next. I was beginning to believe that I would never be able to attain my goal.

I have always loved old sayings. There is one that really applied at that juncture, "Timing is everything." It was a very difficult time to get into medical colleges. This was just at the end of World War II as the veterans were returning home. The G.I. Bill provided fees, and government funds were readily accepted. Of course, those guys should have been placed on priority. Fighting for their country certainly earned them an education. But it didn't make it easier for me when for every request I made for entrance into medical school, I received the same ole song and dance:

"Sorry, we cannot accept you this year."

"We had twelve hundred applications and can accept only sixty."

"Your fee will not be returned."

"Please continue to further your education towards a B.S. degree."

"Try again next year!"

Miami Beach

For four years I had listened to that same song, with different verses. I got to where I could almost tell you what each letter contained before I opened it. Each year I became more and more despondent. I began to enter into, what I would term, a Sinking Spell. I decided I needed to take a year off. After all, if I could not attain the goal I had set for myself, what did I want to do with my life? I entertained the idea of getting a job on the strip at Miami Beach in a hotel.

So, I set out from Valdosta to Miami Beach. I walked from one hotel to another for about five miles. There were no openings. As I entered the Sun and Surf Club, I felt it was just the place I was searching for. I was granted an interview, and everything went along smoothly. The manager felt my southern drawl would be well accepted, and I felt great as he told me the job was mine. As I thanked him and stood up to leave he asked, "You are twenty-one, aren't you?" My heart sank. I wouldn't be twenty-one for a few more months. So much for being a cabana boy at the Sun and Surf. I had to locate a job. Fortunately my Uncle Don was chairman of the board of a concrete plant in Miami. Knowing how hard I had tried to find a job, he decided to really, and I mean really, put me to work. I thought I had been working hard as a lifeguard and teaching swimming lessons. This job was extremely hard physical labor, with very long hours. I was paid one American dollar for an hour's work, and one week I received a paycheck for one hundred and thirty-eight dollars. I realized very soon that I damn sure didn't want any part of this kind of work for the rest of my life.

My uncle had a new night foreman who had a hard time making his own decisions. His telephone rang three or four times every night, as the foreman asked stupid questions. It wasn't long before Uncle Don sent for me. He asked if I would take the night foreman's job. There were only two stipulations. One was that I let him sleep and use my own judgement. The other was that I had to be happy with the same buck an hour.

I took the "promotion". There were thirty-seven men working under me, all of them colored, all of them taking home larger paychecks than I. My uncle wanted no one saying he was showing his nephew partiality, even if I was the foreman.

We generally shut the plant down for an hour each evening to make necessary repairs and ensure the equipment was properly greased. One night I took the grease gun and walked up the rubber belt about one hundred feet in the air to grease some rollers. There was one black guy from Nassau who obviously resented the fact that I had been appointed foreman over him. He knew that I had been taking pre-med courses and sarcastically began calling me Doc. As I was greasing those rollers, he passed by the control switch and turned it on. The conveyor belt began moving, and I was in a very precarious situation. I began yelling; hoping someone would hear me above the noise and realized I had a couple of choices. I could either jump down about fifty-five feet to another roof or be turned into a batch of concrete blocks. Either choice meant disaster. I was very fortunate that someone heard my yells and seeing what was going on, threw the switch just in the nick of time. After that I am sure the black guy from Nassau called me much more than Doc. It certainly wasn't half of what I called him! All of the guys told me he had tried to do away with me, and I never trusted him from then on.

Hit the Road, Jack

As I said, I enjoy old sayings and one of my favorites is, "It doesn't take me long to pick up a hot horse shoe." That year of experience really made me appreciate the collegiate life a wee bit more. I finished my year of hard labor and quickly got the hell out of Dodge. I knew that Brer Rabbit would be happier in his brier patch, so I did like I had been told, "further your education towards a B.S. degree." I majored in Chemistry, with a minor in Biology, and continued sending applications to medical schools. After five years of trying, I was accepted into the Southern College of Pharmacy in Atlanta.

It took three years to finish Pharmacy School. When I began, it seemed that graduation was a long way off and that it would take forever. I studied hard, anxious to finish, get that diploma and begin my career.

It was during my senior year that my father died. It was almost impossible to concentrate on my studies when I returned to college after his funeral. There was a definite void deep in my heart, but I knew that Dad would want me to press on and finish the school I had worked so hard to get into.

On that special day of my life, I had packed my bags and probably left my car engine running. When I was presented my diploma and the usual hand shaking on the platform, I turned around and walked down the aisle and out the front door of the auditorium. I was sitting on ready. I took great pride in my new profession and knew that I was well prepared for my future. In addition to my classes, I worked after school each day in two pharmacies in Atlanta. Working sixty hours a week and going to college made me burn the midnight oil to keep up with my homework. I thought these long hours were over when I graduated, but I was soon to find out that was not the case. I had been offered eighty-six jobs and soon began researching my options. The offers were in cities all over Georgia and Florida. Because both my parents were native Floridians, I was going first to the Sunshine State to check things out.

While traveling south an old college friend popped in my mind. Remembering that he lived in Griffin, Georgia and that I would be driving right through there, I decided to stop and look him up. His wife's family lived in Valdosta, and I had delivered their paper in my paper boy days. Jack, Annie Jean and I had a joyous reunion, and when I told him I was through school and looking for the right place to begin working he said, "Just hold on a minute." He had no intention of letting me leave Griffin, much less go all the way to Florida. A couple of phone calls later my buddy had arranged an interview, and to my delight, I was employed before I knew it. What a true friend!

THE WANDERINGS OF A PILL ROLLER

Experience—the Best Teacher

The owner of the pharmacy where I began working had an assistant in his eighties. He was quite a character. Together the two men had about four years of schooling. I assumed that since I had just completed twice as many years of studies, then I must be twice as smart. Well, I was one hundred percent wrong! It took me through the first paycheck to tell myself, experience is still the best teacher. They were talking about things "I ain't never heard of." In fact, I wondered if we were in the same profession. I began to pay closer attention.

The owner was a perfectionist, and as long as I did every thing his way, I knew I was right. I certainly benefited from his guidance. The green behind my ears began to wash off, and I was well on my way. He molded me into a super good pharmacist. I soon began to feel I was the BEST—my confidence cup ran over. I knew that getting to the top was just a matter of time and patience, and thank God I possessed an abundance of the latter. Courtesy, good manners and respect were well-ingrained traits my parents had instilled in their sons. It paid off in good dividends. The old adage, "You can catch more flies with honey than you can with vinegar," was still true.

After the first year there, the Rotary Club recognized me as being the most courteous sales person in Griffin, Georgia. It was quite an honor when I was presented the Rotary Wheel Award so early in my career. I was off to a great beginning, and I was very thankful. Thirty years later, I was further honored by the Clayton Rotary Club in Clayton, GA with a second Wheel Award for *Service Above Self*. These awards are among my most treasured mementos.

The population of Griffin was near twenty thousand. There were eight drug stores, all downtown. During this era of the late 1950's, there were no neighborhood shopping centers.

In most of the independent pharmacies, procedures were very lax. A lot of over-the-counter prescribing was taking place. The drug inspector would pay a visit a couple of times a year. It was strange, but when he left Atlanta, we seemed to get word that he was on his way. That gave us time to clean up our act.

The main problem occurred when the doctors called in prescriptions in a class required by law to be written out, signed and delivered by the patient to the pharmacy. These were called Class II drugs. Ma Bell was just too convenient. A quick telephone call to the pharmacist and on to the next patient. It took less time to call in the prescription than it did to write it out. I have always felt that the sorrier a doctor scribbled his prescription, the better doctor he was.

When we heard that the inspector was coming, we had to run the doctors down to keep from getting in trouble with unsigned prescriptions. I am sure the inspector knew what was going on, but he had to feel his importance some way.

The inspector would always check a book we called *The Registry*. That was our *Bible*. It was used for controlled drugs that could be sold over-the-counter. Paregoric could be purchased by the ounce, as could certain cough syrups and poisons. There were times when people would come in to see who had bought poison. Someone had done away with their pet. The customers all had to sign the book and give their address.

Some addicts would travel around to different pharmacies purchasing paregoric, not knowing that soon the inspector would be hot on their trails. After all, paregoric contains morphine that could be heated, boiled and evaporated to a residue. Then it could be made into a solution to be injected.

I once went with a doctor friend of mine to a jail where he showed me a man who had used a spoon, a candle, a medicine dropper and a needle for his apparatus to inject morphine. The guards were bringing it to his cell in the form of paregoric, presumably for medicinal purposes. He had told them that he had a bad case of diarrhea, and paregoric was sure to stop it. I could not help but notice this man had a tattoo on his arm—Born to Lose.

I recall a woman who would drive a red pickup truck to town every Saturday. The truck would be loaded with children. The woman would send a child into each pharmacy in town to purchase an ounce of paregoric. Apparently she was pretty well hooked on this substance, and at the end of her trip, she had enough to last until the next Saturday. Then she would come into town again, sending a different child in to make the purchase. It took a few Saturdays, but we finally realized what was happening and cut off her supply.

Almost every morning there would be a group of men waiting for the front doors to be unlocked. They would act as if they had not seen me in a month, when in reality they had just been in the day before. This group of winos must have thought they had found an inexpensive liquor store, because they mainly wanted to purchase a can of sterno. They didn't like the jelly like consistency of the sterno and would take it and filter it through a slice of bread. Their other choices would be Hoyt's cologne, liquid shoe polishes and vanilla extract. None of these were controlled substances and were easily purchased. Sometimes I would read about some of these men in the obituary section of the paper; they didn't last too long on this kind of nourishment.

One colored man came to my store with a prescription that I filled. He returned in a few days and wanted a refill but had left the bottle at home. He said he wanted some more courage pills. I said to him, "What do you mean?" I had no earthly idea what he meant. He replied, "You know, Doc, the ones with Up-John on them."

One of the black men who frequented my store passed out in his bed one evening. He lived across from my business. I happened to look out the window and saw smoke coming out of his house. I dropped everything and ran across the street. He would have suffocated had I not kicked his door open and drug him out of bed to safety. I certainly didn't stop to see what color he was. He was my friend and kept an eye out for my pharmacy as long as he was my neighbor.

Pharmacies or drug stores were vulnerable to being robbed. The owner of the pharmacy where I began my practice had recently been robbed and pistol-whipped by a couple of thugs. The owner was just closing up for the day when two men entered the store. They came around the prescription counter with their pistols drawn. One of them struck the owner and knocked him to the floor. In the early days of my working as a pharmacist, most robberies were not for drugs but for money. Such was the case with these two men. They were later arrested and appeared in court. They were convicted and went to prison for robbery.

One violation of federal regulations that happened with frequency in some pharmacies was the sale of penicillin tablets, not over-the-counter but under-the-counter. There was a high concentration of black people in the area where I practiced and an unbelievable number of venereal disease cases. Penicillin tablets were sold under-the-counter for a dollar and a half per dozen. There was no label used or directions given. They were just placed in a small plain box or bottle. This way there was no means of identification if any problems arose. The customers would pay for the tablets and leave in a hurry so they could begin taking them. They never wanted anyone to think that they were buying them for their own use. They generally asked for them for a friend. Occasionally they would tell us they had picked up the disease from sitting on a toilet. Our standing joke was that this was a heck of a place to take a woman. When I was young, Mama told me to always line the public toilet seats with toilet paper. It was really thought that V. D. might be spread from a toilet seat.

Symptoms of a bad case of V.D. were very obvious. There was a characteristically horrible odor and a pair of yellow tinted blood shot eyeballs. Through awareness of what was happening, stronger controls concerning penicillin were instituted. Health Departments began working to help control this disease, and slowly the under-the-counter sale of penicillin became history.

These were *Steel Magnolia* times for the pharmacist, as he was considered to be the judge and jury. When someone came in needing medicine after the doctors had gone home, they were just as happy for us to go ahead and refill the prescription as we felt was necessary. If the pharmacist felt someone was pushing things a little too far, then it was up to him to tighten up the cinches. Doctors had no way of knowing if patients went to more than one doctor to get certain prescriptions. If the prescriptions were brought to the same drugstore, then an alert pharmacist could detect this.

Doctors were frequently in the lax mode. They were busy getting established. Their secretaries were booking more patients than it was humanly possible for one man to treat. Some few doctors turned the task of calling in their prescriptions over to their staff. Pharmacists would accept these calls but were not thrilled with having to fill prescriptions called in by the secretary or a nurse. There was a slight resentment. A little knowledge could be a dangerous thing. All this was the way of life in a small town, easy going and a kind of live and let live attitude.

Through the years I did see a few physicians bite off more than they could chew. One who comes to memory's eye was very sincere and sympathetic with his patients. He became so concerned and involved, that it proved to be too much for him, and one day all of that hard work caught up with him. Denny had lived and breathed his practice. He pushed himself day and night for so long that he could go no further, and it took my dear friend away.

There was a pathologist who would drop by to see me quite frequently after his day in the office. His family traded with me, and from all appearances everything was going well for them. One night he dropped in and asked if I would fill a prescription for himself. "Sure, that's what I am here for," I answered. He wrote his prescription for Nembutal (a sedative composed of a barbiturate). He told me that he was off the next day and since his family was out of town, he was inviting some of his friends over for a game of poker and wanted me to join them. I was able to make the game, and we had a great time. The game ended about one a.m. The next morning someone found the doctor lying on the bathroom floor. He had overdosed on the Nembutal.

Later I discovered that he had gone to another pharmacy after he had left mine, written another prescription and had it filled there. Even though I had done no wrong, it took awhile to get my emotions in check. The memory of that night of fun at the poker table and the death of my friend comes to mind every now and then. There seemed to be no reason for what happened, or at least none that I ever knew.

The Policewoman

My daughter had begun her education and was now in grade school. I got a big kick out of dropping her off at school on my way to work. I enjoyed watching her and her chums being escorted across the street by a policewoman. I always told the officer, "Good morning," calling her by her first name and frequently stopped to make small talk. She was black, performing her job in an all-white school. She was always so friendly, and I never even thought of her as being black. She was also a very good customer at the pharmacy where I had begun my practice.

Every time she came into the store, she would by-pass the owner and his assistant and wanted me to be the one to fill her prescriptions. Having gained a good deal of respect in a professional manner, I was now titled Dr. Beal by most of the clientele. In fact, pharmacists were rated number two for confidentiality, just behind their preachers.

One day this policewoman came in and as usual asked particularly for me to fill her prescriptions. I remember feeling really good about the situation and the confidence that seemed to be developing between us. I had no idea the events of this day in the late 50's would make an impression in my life that would last forever. As I was making the charges to her account, I noticed that she was taking each bottle and reading the labels. A perplexed look had appeared on her brow. I asked if there was a problem. She then motioned for me to come around the counter, as she wanted to talk to me in privacy. What took place had to be the biggest surprise of my entire profession.

In a complete state of innocence I asked again, "Did I make a mistake?" She began sounding off and abruptly stated, "I am legally married. I have a legal husband. My children aren't bastards! They are also legal."

She went on to say, "I thought you were supposed to type everything on the label that the doctor had written on my prescription." Still communicating with her from a professional standpoint I asked, "What type of mistake did I make on your label?"

Her response floored me. "My name begins with Mrs. and on every label on all of the prescriptions that you have filled, you have omitted the Mrs. I don't know the reason for this, but I want Mrs. typed on my labels."

At the time I wondered if this had something to do with the Gettysburg address. I just could not understand the big problem.

An explosion of time had just erupted. She had ignited the fuse. My Heritage Horse had been unbridled, and I had been taught to ride it by both my parents since I was a boy. This was against my upbringing, against the grain of a lifetime of teaching. I had been pushed into dining on a crow with a slice of humble pie for dessert.

—My mind became a vacuum, suspended in action/reaction.

—My blood pressure rose, while my facial expressions froze.

—My thoughts seemed to be caught up in a mental whirlwind.

—A few hundred years were mentally reflected in just a matter of seconds.

—Then as if it had a voice, my heritage all shouted back at me.

Of course, this woman had no idea what had transpired in my mind and dripped on through my intestinal gut in just a few seconds. It was a mental review of a historical roladex, consisting of my parental guidance and upbringing.

It wasn't a matter of fighting back, as I had nothing really to fight about. I had been around blacks much of my life, and I had never heard of black women being addressed as Mrs. This was a title that they gave to the white folk. Right or wrong, that's just the way it had always been. Now I was confronted with instantaneous change. Two lives were embarking on a new road to an unknown destination. We were both propelled by the winds of time.

When all of the evolutionary dust had settled and composure regained, I took her bag of prescriptions and began retyping. I inhaled a very deep breath to become relaxed. I let her know that she could return the labels on any of her other prescriptions, and I would re-do those also. There is no way of explaining how hard it was for me to bite the bullet and to also bite my tongue while I turned my cheek. I let her know that I was not happy with the way she brought this to my attention in such an abrupt manner. Deep inside I was torn between the cultural changes that were being forced upon me.

I was a professional, at her service and had no intentions of hurting her feelings. I wanted her to be confident in my abilities, but I also wanted her to see where I was coming from and know what I felt. The problem was she had no idea what I was thinking and had no reason to care.

I realized that her family physician had been writing her prescriptions. I had been referring patients of both races to this new black doctor who had just arrived in order to help build his practice. He was a good physician, and I certainly didn't mind helping him get established in his new practice. Griffin's black population was increasing, and there was a great need for this new doctor. Some black residents would now have a choice and might prefer his services to others.

It was customary for pharmacists to label medicine as the prescription was written by the doctor. I cannot ever recall seeing a prescription for black customers being made out as Mr. or Mrs. This was a first for me. The doctor was only showing respect for his patients by addressing them as Mr. or Mrs. I wouldn't even give it a second thought in today's time.

It was a way of life to not refer to a black man or woman as a Mr. or Mrs. It definitely was not intended as a slight. It was the way things were done back then. But because of that incident, a cloud was thrown over the friendship between the policewoman and me. Each time we encountered one another after that incident, our relationship was just not the same.

INTEGRATION

Southern Winds at a Gale Force

One of the most obvious changes that began developing was in conversations with black children. Throughout all of my growing up years, I had been taught to respect my elders. It was natural for my older brother, Jimmie, and me to use sir and ma'am. We would not have dreamed of addressing adults otherwise. Most of the children looking over my counters had been taught the same as I.

Now there was a drastic change. It was as if someone had instructed, "Say this no more my children. From now on you can leave it off. This denotes servitude, and you are not their servants." In many cases they were told, "You don't have to think you are not as good as white folk. You are better than they are." Saying sir and ma'am was a courtesy denoting respect and good manners. This was something that had been done by all children, black and white, and it was distasteful to watch this disappear. Sometimes I would hear a child slip and say the *word*. If they said yes, then a hiss followed as they cut off the sir or ma'am. And if they began the word sir, it would be cut off sounding like six S's had just come out of their mouths. It took only a short while for this new way to become instilled, and sir and ma'am swiftly began to disappear from their vocabulary.

Other ways of life began changing. The city park and municipal golf course were located only a couple of blocks from my pharmacy.

Sometimes I felt they were too close and on beautiful days seemed to beckon me from my work. At that time blacks were not allowed either in the pool or to play golf. The caddies were allowed a free round once a week in the evening when all the whites had finished playing. Two of my favorite caddies were named Boots and Mac. We had many memorable rounds walking the eighteen holes together.

Plans began evolving for the integration of the city pool. I played golf quite often with the Mayor, and when he called to cancel our golf game the next day, I asked him what was going on. Somehow the news had gotten out that the time had arrived; several blacks were planning to attempt to enter the pool the next afternoon. The mayor and the City Council held an emergency meeting, with one item on the agenda. That night the pool was completely filled with dirt and rocks, then a substance called concrete was applied to the surface. No one could believe what had transpired. There was no swimming for anyone except in the creeks. The pool surface was soon laid out and became basketball courts. These were quickly taken over by the young black men in the community.

For the next few years, I would say that all hell began breaking loose. Racial unrest had begun its course, and integration was thrust upon us like a plague. No one had any idea what to expect. This was in the early days of television, and we watched in horror and disbelief at the scenes of confrontation, sit-in's and beatings. These things were happening not only in my little town of Griffin but all across the South.

People I had known, worked with and cared about for years were suddenly demanding to be treated differently. The ways of living and thinking that we had grown up with, our values and customs, were being challenged. Change was demanded overnight, and as we all know, change is hard to accept and even more so when it is thrust upon you and required. When that happens it is human nature to raise our hackles, dig in even deeper and hold our ground.

The Russians Weren't Coming, But the Molotovs Arrived

In 1961 I felt I had gained enough experience and confidence, not to mention the nest egg I had sacrificed to accumulate, to open my own pharmacy. It was located right in the middle of a black community about a block from the hospital. There were many very small, shoebox size houses that rented mostly by the week. Property values began going up rapidly because of the proximity to the hospital, and many of these rental homes were being torn down to make room for new medical offices that were locating in that area. I thought this would be a prime location and was right. After a period of time, there were over thirty doctors surrounding my new pharmacy.

But before these houses were torn down, and during the turbulent, beginning days of racial unrest, the tension became so great that the need to be ready to protect my store caused me to plan ahead.

A new cocktail began showing up in my small town and in many other towns across the South. It was known as a molotov. This had nothing to do with the Russians. It was very simple to concoct. Locate an empty bottle like an R C or liquor. Fill it full of kerosene, and stuff a rag down in it for a wick. Just bust out a plate glass window with a rock and after adding a flame to the wick, let it fly. Get behind a tree and watch the boom.

There were a couple of cocktails tossed into a hardware store located near the tracks. Every item therein was charred or melted beyond recognition. It was hard to understand why that store was targeted. The clientele was mostly black, and it was well known that the owner had been very accommodating to all the families in that neighborhood for many years. Although he was a white man, he had the reputation of being courteous and understanding to everyone, carrying some of their accounts when times were hard.

The bombing of this store was a causative agent of a tremendous fear that swallowed up the city. All of the business owners wondered who would be next. This was a very tense time for all of us. Our small, lazy town had become a mini war zone.

It became prudent for me to keep a loaded pistol behind the counter, pointed at whomever was directly in front of me. I knew that the bad guys had the advantage. They knew what they planned to do, and I didn't. However, I felt a little more mentally secure by being prepared and would not have hesitated to use that pistol p.r.n. (as needed).

My family and I had made many sacrifices in order that I might go into business for myself, and I was not just going to stand by and let it be blown away or messed with.

Sleeping With the Enemy, But Where Is It?

So, I began setting up my camp and would return to my new quarters each night around ten. There, behind the prescription counter in the same tracks where I had stood on my feet working all day, I rolled out my sleeping bag on an air mattress. Beside it I placed a deer rifle and twelve gauge automatic shotgun and strapped my thirty-eight revolver on my side. I didn't want to have to use them but had decided that if that is what it took to defend what belonged to me, then I would do so.

With working from early morn through dark, going home only to eat dinner, it didn't matter where I lay my tired body down. I would try to keep one eye open and rest the other while listening carefully for a change in nocturnal sounds. I kept the store completely in darkness. The only lights to dimly break the blackness came from a few stores or doctor's offices nearby.

One of my black friends had told me, "Doc, ain't nobody goin in yo sto when dey gotta strike a match to see."

As night after night passed with no trouble at my store, I began to believe he was absolutely correct. In fact, I began to relax just a little and occasionally got a few hours sleep. I even toyed with the idea of staying at home and sleeping in a real bed.

Nocturnal Sounds

Then one night, just as I settled down and began to nod off, I detected noises that were not normal and slipped up to my rooftop to get a closer look at the situation. About a block away was a neighborhood grocery. It too was owned and operated by a white man, but most of the blacks in the neighborhood traded with him. I knew that he was not in the store that night and figured I needed to slip through the shadows to check out what was happening. As I neared his store, the voices grew louder. There was a lot of profanity. A couple of guys seemed to be the leaders and were feverishly stirring up the others with accusations and reasons why the grocery store should be the next to be fire bombed.

Slowly and cautiously I began backing off and when I felt the way was clear, I did an about face and ran quickly back to my store. A call to the police, to let them know what was in the making, was interrupted by sounds of glass breaking and soon the loud noise of sirens in the distance. I told the officer that it was too late. The grocery store was demolished, and the owners never bothered to open it again. Just a short time later a house was burned, then another.

There were many sleepless nights for me during these trying times. I went through holy hell trying to take care of my business during the day and protect it at night. The sleeping bag became a way of life, as a rash of break-ins began to develop all over town. This finally forced most of us to go to the expense of having an alarm system installed. Even at that there were many nights that the storeowners had to play the role of vigilante. The police even loaned us walkie-talkies so that we could stay in touch. We became their helpers and did a lot of good many nights either helping to prevent break-ins or destruction. At times we were able to aid in the capture of those participating in these acts.

R & R

Occasionally I got a chance to get away for rest and recreation. About thirty-five miles due east of Griffin, Georgia was one of my favorite locations for a little R & R. It served me much better than an appointment with a psychologist.

Jackson Lake provided me with many happy moments through the years. It was constructed in 1910 and witnessed many historical times.

The dam is located on the Ocmulgee River that contains four tributaries. One of my favorite areas was the Tussehaw River. Each time I motored under Barnett's Bridge which crossed this river, I was reminded of stories that were told to me about times when colored men crossed the race line. When they were accused of raping a white girl, they were escorted to Barnett's Bridge. From there the violator was chained and pushed into the water never to be seen again. Without question their accusers became judge, jury and executioners. This was not the only bridge that was used for this purpose of punishment throughout the South during the early 1900's.

The white folks all across the South just could not accept this violation of their human rights. Now, when I think of these stories, I am appalled. Back then it was just a way of life.

Dining With Who?

One weekend four of us took a couple of boats to fish in Lake Sinclair, a beautiful lake near Milledgeville, Georgia. We got there in time to get the boats launched before daylight, but one boat spurted and sputtered and would not start. We had engine trouble and left it with a mechanic at the marina who indicated he could quickly fix it. We decided to go to town and eat breakfast. We were all starving and were in search of a big man's breakfast. There was only one café open at that hour. When we arrived, it looked strange that there were two entrance doors. As we got closer, we saw why. While there was no sign indicating this, all of the black people were entering one door and the white people the other. Inside was a horseshoe bar and grill with the cash register at the front.

This must have been a very popular place, as it was crowded. Several black men were perched on stools eating their breakfast across from us. They were dressed like workmen, and because of the area we were in, we thought they might be getting ready to go out into the pinewoods to empty the turpentine buckets from the pine trees. This was and still is one of the main businesses in that area.

I knew that it would be difficult for me to enjoy my meal while watching the table manners displayed by this group of men. Looking at each other in dismay, we decided our hunger would overcome our distaste, and proceeded to order ham, grits and eggs along with pancakes. But as we waited for our food, we began to have second thoughts. I guess I was the first to cancel my order, and the others decided to follow. We just took a bottle of milk and a sack full of cinnamon rolls and went out to the curb to eat and discuss the matter.

This was a first for all of us, and we never stopped talking about it the entire day. We just could not understand why we had such a change come over us. We all felt as if we had invaded the privacy of those men. If that was the way they wanted to eat, it was their business, but it seemed to strongly go against the grain of our upbringing. As we talked we found it was the first time any of us had eaten with black people. Those who had been a part of our household for many years had always preferred to eat alone.

The next time I encountered a similar situation I was in Atlanta and decided to eat at the now closed S & W Cafeteria. This was a great, inexpensive place to eat. The food was wonderful, and it was always extremely busy. There was a table of black people near us. They all wore nice suits and dresses. Table manners had certainly been taught in their homes, because they used their napkins properly, had good manners and spoke distinctly. I soon forgot they were there and thoroughly enjoyed my meal.

Integration was beginning to take hold in the South. My first two encounters of sharing a meal with black people were as different as day and night. As I drove home I thought about how things were changing, and I pondered where all this was going. I also thought about the fact that there were a whole lot of white folks that I wouldn't enjoy dining with. There were different cultures, different upbringings and different people. Our world was fast changing, and there surely had to be a way for everyone to live and work together. In my world there had always seemed to be a sense of harmony and balance. But now it seemed as if there were changes thrust upon us everyday, some subtly, and others blowing across the South with the force of tornadoes.

Susie

I thought about Susie, a maid who worked in our home for over twenty years. She was a dear person, not real easy to get close to, but undeniably a friend after she got to know me. She had a pug nose with freckles that danced across her face when she laughed, which was often. She wore outfits that looked like uniforms, with her hair covered always with a net or a cap. She was an integral part of my family and was loved by all. Bless her heart, she is gone now, but I know she will never be forgotten. The only time the "N" word was ever used in our house was when Susie said it. She had gotten her dander up about someone that really upset her and was telling me about it.

Susie raised both my children as if they were her own. They loved her like another mother. Sometimes at night I would enjoy going to my club to play a little poker. If I had a productive evening at that game of chance, I would share my winnings with Susie the next morning. This was more or less a little extra, like a tip, for her being so nice to the family. This little deal was just between Susie and me, and no one else ever knew our secret. She always said to me, "Lawsey me, Mr. Everett, you are a bugger, thank you much." She appreciated any favors that came her way. There was mutual love and respect between Susie and me.

I can remember my mother telling her some story, and Susie would say, "Uh huh, uh huh," while paying close attention to what was being said.

Susie loved her snuff and enjoyed a pinch that protruded in her bottom lip. I can't remember ever seeing her spit. She cooked some wonderful meals for us, and after serving them in the dining room, she would eat at the kitchen table. That was the way she wanted it. This came from her heritage, well in-grained in her everyday life, and passed on down to her children and grandchildren.

As others in her race were pushing for change, Susie often made comments to me that she thought they ought to just leave things alone. She didn't have no truck with them that was making all the trouble. Susie remained a wonderful, trusted friend and a dear person.

Just as Susie had her heritage and ways of doing things and living, so did we, the white folks. Changes never come easy, and during the 60's change seemed to be expected and demanded. This was the basis for much of the unrest and many of the problems seen during that time.

What Would You Do?

My preacher resided across the street from me in Griffin. He was very sports minded and enjoyed golf and tennis. He did very well in tennis. Once he made the finals, though, he had to withdraw. They were to be played on a Sunday afternoon, and he felt it would not be right for him to be playing then. You have to remember that things were a little different in the 60's. He also did quite a bit of jogging in his back yard. This was before jogging became such a popular activity. He felt a little sensitive about his congregation seeing him jogging on the streets.

I played quite a lot of golf and tennis with my friend and even jogged around his back yard trail when I could find the time. Once in a while he would prepare for us one of the best steaks I have ever eaten. I never could find out just what he did to make them so great. I wonder if trying to keep up with him on his jogging trail for a couple of miles did something to my appetite.

He was a great friend. We had many lively discussions about the issues of that day and time. Once when we really got deep into the subject of integration, a subject uppermost in the minds of most people in those days, he decided to call a spade a shovel, (another of my sayings).

He asked me, "Everett, what would you do if one day you were ushering and some black people decided to attend our services?" I assumed that he already had the answer, so I said, "You tell me, what would I do?" "How about a stroll with these nice people down the middle aisle of the auditorium to the front row seat so they could enjoy my sermon," he replied. I never had any takers but was ready if that should happen.

Because of the actions of some, it seemed that all blacks were believed to be bad, and that was not fair. Nor was it true any more than the assumption that all whites should be lumped into the category of being mean and uncaring to the blacks.

When things seemed to be getting quieter, I ceased spending all my nights at the store. It seemed disgusting and degrading to me that I had invested and sacrificed eight years of my life learning how to be a pharmacist and five more on experience. And in order to protect what was mine, I had to sleep on the floor. That could also explain some of the animosity that is within me for those who made these protective measures a necessity.

DRUGS

Paving the Way to Mulatto Street

In the early 1970's, just as our streets seemed to quiet down a little and a calmer acceptance of integration settled upon us, another insidious event reared its ugly head. It seems that the illicit use of drugs started its rapid rise. I was asked by the local drug enforcement officials to go on some raids with them. They needed my expertise in identifying any drugs they might find that were supposed to be obtained by prescription only. I saw what was happening from pushers getting kids hooked on drugs. A two-story house in town had been rented and taken over by two black men. They had quite a setup in that house. Marijuana and cocaine, blended in with uppers and downers, were found in abundance. It was a haven for illegal and illicit business. They had pornographic movies playing. There were several white girls there that had been kept on a high through drugs, and their bodies were being sold to anyone willing to pay a few bucks. These girls were their white slaves, and because of the drugs they didn't know what they were doing or who was doing it to them. The prostitution and the drugs that were sold helped the men to make bundles of money.

I wanted to see these guys put under the jail. It would not have made a difference to me if the girls had been black girls. This was a terrible destruction of any human's life. It became more and more common to find the combination of white girls and black guys as houses like this were raided. It seemed that the roads were all leading to just one street—Mulatto Street.

When I saw what was behind the doors that were kicked open by the drug enforcement people, it made me sick to my guts. The girls being used there turned into nobodies. Their thoughts of reasons were stripped from them by drugs.

Once my store was broken into during the nocturnal hours, and some drugs were taken. Even though the individual was later apprehended, there did not seem to be enough evidence to convict him. A few days later this person had the audacity to come into my store with a prescription to be filled. I looked up with anger and almost crawled over the counter when I typed his name on the label.

As I handed him the medicine, I said, "Thanks for doing business with me during open hours rather than when the doors are locked and I am trying to sleep." I will never forget his reply. "Sorry about that. I didn't know what I was doing. I was on a high."

Life became a little easier for me when I employed another pharmacist to work with me. There were still a few break-ins that occurred; the difference being that now they were drug related. Because the culprits knew which bottles to take, the ones with the highest street value, and even knew where they were located; we began storing certain drugs in secret compartments. But somehow they stayed one jump ahead of us.

It was rumored among pharmacists that there was a special type of drug school these crooks could go to in Alabama. They learned the tricks of their trade like the switch and what to look for when they broke into a pharmacy. I never knew this for sure, but they sure did know what to take and what to leave when they broke into the stores.

Another thing that began to be rampant, and still is a terrible factor in the war on drugs today, was the sale of these drugs to children. Being a pharmacist I know the beneficial and necessary value of drugs administered correctly through the auspices of a physician. I also have seen the complete destruction of the minds and bodies of those who abuse drugs.

To hear of persons who take it upon themselves to ruin lives of children in order that they might make money is totally incomprehensible.

With the number of crimes happening, there developed a very serious distrust for black males. People began to be apprehensive and sometimes more than a little nervous just because they came into the room. There were many over-the-shoulder, second glances, especially while standing in a rest room at a urinal. I do not mean to imply that only black people were involved in the drug crimes, for that is not true. But at that time, in the city where I lived, this was predominantly a crime committed by blacks.

The greatest enemy the black man and I share is drugs. I have now seen this crime over half of my life, and I have abhorred the destruction of human beings of all races. I have seen what uncontrolled drugs can do. I would like to see any drug pusher strung up by their whatchacallits. I know of thousands of lives that have ruined because of this horrible addiction.

A Very Close Call

During the time I worked after hours with the drug enforcement agents, I saw doors kicked off their hinges leaving the passage wide open as we entered a place where there was suspicion of drugs. Once they left me in the living room of a house to keep an eye on a guy that they had told to stay seated on the sofa while they checked out the house for other people or drugs. They had not taken the time to handcuff the guy I was guarding, and I noticed he seemed to be fumbling for something behind him. I called for one of the officers, who found a twelve-inch butcher knife in the sofa cushions just inches from his hand. This guy was planning to make a break through the open door and take a part of me on the way out. I had been donating my services to the narcs but figured this had been too close for comfort. We found other ways that I could be of service to them in safer surroundings.

Pushers have thrived on getting to many of our athletes and hooking them on their tastes of honey. The excitement of hallucinating and sexual encounters helped form the habit. Many professionals have ruined their futures, and we hear about this happening with great frequency.

I was extremely upset when I would come across those in my profession who got hooked on drugs. This was not a frequent thing, but it did happen. Some physicians would knowingly overprescribe certain drugs to patients, and soon they would be hooked. The very largest quantity I ever saw the drug Percodan prescribed at one time was 48 tablets. Under normal conditions 12, 24 or maybe 36 tablets would be prescribed. Most doctors were very careful not to hook any of their patients on this very habit forming drug. They had great respect for it and all of the Class II drugs. However, I recall one physician passing out prescriptions for Percodan like it was a sack full of peas. It created monsters out of some of his patients, as they began to get hooked on this drug. They had to return to the doctor in order to get another prescription, and this added another charge to their bill. That is the only possible reasoning behind such an action, and under no circumstances could it ever be described as an excuse.

After those who were not strong enough to kick the habit got on his *hallucinatory dreamboat,* we began to see many character changes. It made perpetual liars out of them. We heard:

"Lost my prescription, need more."

"Dropped tablets in commode, need more."

"Someone stole my prescription, need more."

"Lost my luggage on plane, need more."

There began to be several lawsuits against this doctor, and we were all happy to see him leave the country.

There were times when lawyers depended on me to enlighten them on the action/reaction of certain drugs as they prepared their cases.

This often meant that I would testify in court. If you have ever been a witness in a trial, you know that sometimes you have to just sit there for hours or even a day or so before you are called. I had to pay another pharmacist when I was away. The case against an offender would be strong, and I would be so sure that this time the offender would be behind bars. But days later I would see him/her strolling down the sidewalks. The legal system just didn't seem to come out on the winning side very often.

John Paul's Hit List

Some physicians were so busy that they only had the time to quickly diagnose the symptoms of a patient, prescribe or have the nurse give them a shot and make an appointment for a return visit if needed. Normally there was very little time to chew the fat and get to know the patients.

I was busy as a one-legged-man in a butt kicking contest trying to keep up with all the business and make everybody happy. It came back to me that I had once thought the long hours would be over when I finished school. But I seemed to thrive on being busy. I tried to have some time to talk with my patrons. One day a blond haired gentleman came into the store. He had on a navy blue short sleeved shirt, and a tattoo showed on his arm. I happened to look up as the sun reflected on the new red Chevy he parked outside the store and noticed that he was from Tennessee. He came in and inserted his prescription into the group I was working on. He sat down at a bay window on the red deacon's bench. Our town was still small enough that strangers were recognized, especially strangers with a prescription from a local doctor driving a beautiful new red car like one I had admired down at the local Chevy dealer.

When I got around to his prescription, I could not help but notice the address he had given the doctor was up in North Georgia. The prescription called for thirty-six Dilaudid tablets. This was a Class II drug, a very habit forming one that pushers loved to get in an addict's system. The man's name was John Paul Knowles. He was not too tall and weighed around one hundred fifty pounds. Since his address was in north Georgia, and he was driving a car with Tennessee plates, I began to smell a rat and decided to call the doctor. I asked him if he meant to prescribe that many tablets.

The doctor said, "Sure, I meant to prescribe that many tablets. Why are you asking?" I told him of the discrepancy in the address and car tag.

He replied, "He is a super nice fellow on his way to the motorcycle races in Daytona Beach. I had time to talk with him, and he has a type of facial paralysis. Dilaudid seems to be the only drug that relieves the pain, and he forgot and left his at home. He's okay. Don't worry about it—a good guy."

This doctor was a little different from some others. He would often take time for conversation to entertain himself. He had his secretary book just the number of patients he wanted to see in order not to be rushed and overdo it.

I still had reservations, but filled the prescription as directed and watched John Paul drive away.

About an hour later a dentist friend of mine called and asked, "What the hell is Dilaudid?" He said he had a patient named John Paul Knowles who claimed that Dilaudid was the only drug that would tide him over 'til he got to Jacksonville, Florida to see his dentist. He said he had facial neuralgia and could not bear the pain without this medication. I told the dentist what had transpired and asked him to keep John Paul there as long as possible and if he had to, only write a prescription for a few tablets. I wanted him to delay as long as he could so that I could get the police to check out this fellow. It was over a half-hour before the officer arrived, and by that time John Paul was gone. That evening a doctor friend and I drove through all of the motel parking lots nearby trying to see if Knowles' car was there. Finally, about two a.m., we called it a night. Information about him was passed to sur-rounding pharmacies and law enforcement personnel.

A few months later John was driving up highway 75 near McDonough, Georgia. A deputy sheriff pulled him over for some traf-fic violation. John was slick. He somehow over-powered the officer and took his weapon. He fled on foot but trespassed on the wrong farmer's land. I was told that John was terminated from both blasts of the farmer's double-barreled shotgun.

A Jacksonville, Florida paper printed quite a story of the life and times of John Paul Knowles. He was suspected of murdering nineteen women while on a rampage across the South. He had been holed up in a motel in Jacksonville for a couple of weeks with an English woman who was writing a book. Apparently he was very fond of her and left her to write her novel. I never found out if that book was ever published, but if she were aware of John Paul's scheming ways, it could have filled many pages in her book.

Sometimes it did pay for me to be cautious. I let the doctor know about his good friend John Paul Knowles and what a little Dilaudid could make one do.

Always on the Lookout

One night, just before closing time, a couple of suspicious looking characters came into my store. One remained up front while the other asked me to fill a prescription that called for Dilaudid. I readily detected that it was a forgery and on a stolen prescription blank. By their demeanor I felt they were pros and knew what they were doing. It was a touchy situation. I had to make the right decision in how to handle them. I could have just filled the prescription, let them go on their way, try to get their tag number and inform the police. But I knew their chances of getting away were great. The lady who worked at the front register had no way of knowing what was going on. It seemed that both guys were nervous and fidgety. The one up front kept looking outside as if he were checking on something.

If I had told the one asking for the drug that I was temporarily out of it, I didn't know what his reaction would be. I decided to go on and fill the prescription and try to get the police on their trail.

While I was counting out the tablets, he interrupted me to ask how much it would cost. He then walked up front to pay and walked out the door. The other guy came to the back and took the bag. He rushed out the door and to the side street where they had parked their car. I ran as fast as I could to see his tag. They scratched off, but I memorized the numbers and called the police. A couple of days later the two were arrested in a South Carolina motel. In their possession they had eighty thousand pep pills, I was told later. I know it is better to opt for the safest way of handling fake prescriptions, but I was glad I was able to detect the fraud, get their license and be able to aid in their arrest.

In the 60's it seemed that Dilaudid was very much in demand by the pushers. The wholesale cost was a little over thirty dollars for a bottle of a hundred tablets. I sold them for about fifty or sixty cents each, depending on the quantity prescribed. I did not stock a large quantity, because I seldom got a prescription for them.

When a low life would get his hands on them, he could sell one tablet for sixty-five dollars. Think about it. That's sixty-five hundred dollars a bottle. That is why there seems to be such an imbalance in this world. Here I, along with thousands of other pharmacists, worked hard, sometimes sacrificing our lives in order to try and make a living and enjoy some of the many good things life has to offer. And some crooks can steal a bottle of pills, make one hundred percent profit, with no overhead and pay no taxes. I guess that's why drugs have become America's number one problem. Too many people are out to get something for nothing.

Sometimes thieves would steal a big bottle of nitroglycerine (used for problems with the heart). These were called H.T.'s or hypodermic tablets. We wondered why they were being stolen so frequently. We found out that they closely resembled another H.T. tablet of equal size, like morphine. The junkies buying the morphine tablets would play the palm game and switch in a few of the nitroglycerin tablets. They were sharp crooks, and pushers weren't aware of what had been done.

Road to Riches?

Through my years as a pharmacist, I probably reported at least a hundred forged prescriptions, possibly many more. Very few times did the culprit get punished for the crime, at least not for very long. Before stricter rules for maintaining prescription pads were put into effect, it was easy for people to confiscate whole books of prescription blanks from emergency rooms. It was usual for these to be kept handy for the doctors to save time in writing prescriptions, and for years this had not proved to be a problem. Tighter security measures were taken. The pharmacies began a pyramid hot line. A call to one would be relayed to another, and so on down the line. Today this is easy with computers that help keep up with the drugs an individual uses throughout the state. But this was before computers, and we all worked together to get the word out when there was something suspicious going on. We had our own *code red* then, and in a matter of minutes many pharmacists were alerted and on the watch.

There was a female doctor located in Atlanta who had a specialty clinic. It was special alright. She kept prescribing two certain drugs to her patients—Ionamin (a type of amphetamine normally used for dieting) and Valium. One was the upper and the other the downer.

I began to see more and more of her patients bringing their prescriptions to be filled. I loved the business, and it seemed these folks were coming out of the woodwork. One evening I received a call from this doctor. She asked me how I liked all the business she was sending my way. I told her that I appreciated it very much. She then told me that I had better stock up more and more of these two drugs so that I would not run out. "Just keep on taking care of my patients, and I will make you rich," she said.

Anything that sounds too good to be true usually is. I made a quick call to the Drug Enforcement Office, and they paid her a visit the next day. They broke up her *housekeeping* and burst my bubble. I wanted to get rich but not that way, and it gave me a sense of satisfaction knowing that I had done the right thing.

GIVING BACK

Good Ole Dr. Beal

I have always loved working with and being around children and young people. For years I served as Scoutmaster for an Explorer Scout Post consisting of fifty active, busy boys. During that time I learned a lesson I remember well today. That is, time is more valuable than money. Occasionally, I would have to ask some of the parents to help me out on some project or to take over if an emergency kept me from being at a meeting. We had hayrides and camping trips, and extra help was frequently needed. Almost always the answer was that they just did not have the time, but if I needed money they would be glad to write a check. We could have used the donations, but the more critical need was for help.

With the necessity for both parents to be working today, volunteerism is declining even more. If you have the opportunity and can squeeze out the time from busy schedules, don't hesitate to help out in areas where there is need. I can guarantee you will feel a sense of satisfaction that will far exceed that of just writing a check. My days of working with those boys are still treasured memories.

I also taught a Sunday school class for several years. In order to get the teenagers there, I would donate a Timex watch to the one with the most perfect attendance. You might say I bribed them into coming, but hey, you can't offer drink until you get the horse to water. Another watch was given for the one studying his lessons the most. I had the best attendance of the whole department every year. I usually had the captain and co-captain of the football team in my class along with many of the team members. It took some preparation to correlate the lessons with everyday life. By blending in some of the stories of my outdoor activities, I never had a problem holding their attention.

It was important for me to instill into their minds that if they would learn right from wrong and be able to make a distinction between the two, they would then know the right trail they should be hiking and could always find their way back to that trail. Sins committed while hiking other trails could be forgiven, if they remembered and got back on the right trail. I remain in contact with some of those students today and have been told that my simple way of explaining things meant a lot to them.

I hired several high school students to work in my pharmacy over the years. There would be a couple of courteous, pretty girls working out front and at least one guy in the stockroom to check in orders and run errands. This was good training for them, and they were very helpful to me. About half the girls were cheerleaders, and with them working at the store and so many of the ball players in my Sunday school class, you can bet I frequented the high school athletic events. It was with a sense of pride that I watched these young people make progress in the development of their personalities and communication skills with my customers. They were from all walks of life, and it was a great experience for them. Most of them worked a year or two during the summers, and during the school year they were there after school hours and on Saturdays. I had mixed emotions when they left for college, but when they were home on holidays, most would return to work in the pharmacy so they could pick up a few extra bucks.

If at all possible, I said yes when I was asked to be a guest speaker at the high school during Vocation Day. I would give a talk about my profession and got a big kick out of doing my part on the program.

Hopefully, I was instrumental in guiding some of these young people in the right direction.

Elbow Grease

As I think on and remember some of the experiences I had with young black people, several come to mind.

One evening a little black girl came in to replace my porter for a few days. While mopping the floor, with very weak strokes, I told Leslie that she needed to use some elbow grease. The floor was just not getting clean. She laid the mop down and went to the stockroom. After about ten minutes, I walked back to see what was going on. She was looking over all the shelves. I asked her what in the world she was doing.

She said, "I's lookin' for de elbow grease, Dr. Beal. Where is it?" She must have been a direct descendent of Prissie in *Gone With the Wind*. She was so cute.

Rx—Gone With the Wind

Once Clark Gable came into my pharmacy. This one was a little black boy who came in just before noon one day. He said he was hungry and asked if I would give him some money to buy a hamburger. I decided to give Clark a job of sweeping the floor and emptying out trash. I told him to load the trash into the *empty* boxes in the stockroom and then put them in the Dempsey Dumpster out back. After Clark finished his work, I patted him on the back, gave him his pay and told him that he did a good job. He turned as he was leaving and said, "Good ole Dr. Beal" and went on his merry way.

I had been very busy all day and when quitting time came, I was looking forward to going home and resting my feet. As I was closing the doors, a customer hurriedly came up and asked if she was too late. Her prescription was for an item that had just come in that morning and had not yet been unpacked, checked and put on the shelf. I told her it would be a few minutes while I got her medication from the shipment in the back.

When I opened the stockroom door, I was surprised to see the floor was clean as a pin. I looked around for my shipment of medicines, and when I could not locate it, the whereabouts hit me like a ton of bricks. When I regained my senses and returned from the ceiling, I told the customer it would be a little longer. Apparently the boxes I needed were in the Dempsey Dumpster. I rolled up my sleeves and proceeded to dive into the container.

I shared the dumpster with a restaurant next door, and of course, they had emptied their garbage cans on top of the boxes for which I was searching. I can vividly remember clawing through their leftovers, chicken and steak bones, rice and gravy, potato peelings, coffee grounds and other indescribable things that had been emptied that day. And as my luck would have it, the temperature had been over ninety degrees almost all day. It took most of an hour before I found the boxes I needed. Then I had to go to the bathroom and practically take a bath before I could take a very deep breath. After apologizing for the delay, I filled her prescription.

There is more to this story. The very next day, about the very same time, my little friend, Clark Gable, comes into the store and wants to *hep out* and make a little more money. I let Clark know what he had done for me the day before. I even told him about diving into that dumpster searching for those boxes. And then I told him that I was going to close my eyes like I hadn't seen him, turn around real slow and that if I were him, it would be a very good idea that he not be there when I opened my eyes. In fact, it would probably be nice if good ole Dr. Beal never saw him again. I never did see my Clark Gable again, but I often saw his brother around town. He was named Joe Lewis. To this day nausea overcomes me as I remember the hour I spent in the Dempsey Dumpster.

Occasionally, a black child would drop into the pharmacy, we figured just to brighten up our day. I had one little fellow walk up to my counter the very first day that I opened. He said, "I wants a quarters worth of mullet." I really hated to refuse one of my very first customers, but the grocery was in the next block.

Once in a while I would glance over at the sink on the end of my counter to watch my cosmetician lift a child by his armpits. She was having him wash off the coins that he had taken out of his mouth to pay for his purchase. I figured they thought it would be safer from other children if they hid it in their mouths.

Wake Up Calls

During the years I ran my pharmacy, I never refused to return for any emergency. Sometimes, however, I wished I had not returned. The strangest wake-up call I ever received came from a woman around two o'clock one morning. She said she needed to have some prescriptions filled. Since the pharmacy was on her way home from the hospital, I assumed that she had been to the emergency room. So I told her I would be right on down. It would take me about ten minutes to get there.

When I unlocked the door and let her in, and we made our way back to the prescription department, I told her I was sorry that she was having problems. When I turned the corner and flipped on the lights, I noticed she was lining up eight bottles on the counter to be refilled. The first label I looked at read, "take one at bedtime as needed for sleep." There were absolutely no new prescriptions! I guess my explosion woke up the Country Club. I told her very loudly that I was open all the day before and would open again at a decent hour that morning. I also told her that while I appreciated her business, I could not understand how she had the nerve to get me out of the bed at two o'clock in the morning for refills!

She replied, "Honey, I've been so busy all day and half the night. I can't plan my hours. I have to get it when it's coming around."

She was a prostitute, and quickly I understood. When she got ready to pay me she said, "Sweetie pie, I'll either pay you, or you can take it out in trade."

When I told her I preferred cash, she laid on the counter a very large, black pocketbook with a gold catch on it. Then she proceeded to unload the following items: a switchblade, a pair of brass knucks, a pearl handled snub-nosed thirty-eight and a wad of bills that would choke a mule. I decided that I shouldn't say anything else. I took my money and quickly escorted her out the door.

The second most memorable call back to the pharmacy at night was from a doctor at the midnight hour. He asked if I would please come in. It was an emergency. I jumped up and drove as fast as I could to the store. As he followed me back to the prescription department, I heard him chuckling all the way. I asked him what he needed and he said, "Don't you classify prophylactics as an emergency?" It was very hard for me to see any humor in that at the time, and the diatribe I laid on him was much stronger than I could give most of my customers.

My Feets Done Carried Me This Far

There was a delightful colored woman who traded with me, a very good customer, and she always left me laughing. She once told me of a time when she picked a hundred pounds of cotton everyday. She was strong as a mule. Her name was Rosa. She weighed about 250 pounds and was a good six feet three inches tall.

She told me about a time when she walked from Albany, in south Georgia to Griffin. Now if you look at a map, you will see that is quite a distance. I don't know how many days she had been walking, but she had only about seven miles left on her trek when an elderly couple pulled off the highway and said, "Auntie, would you like a ride?"

Rosa looked ahead at the hot road, looked back at them as if she were undecided, and then said, "No, thank you white folks. My feets done carried me this far. I'm gonna let 'em carry me on the rest of the way."

Hey Doc, Can You Stop This Coffin?

Another story I recall being told was about an old colored fellow who had lived out more than his time. He had been well funeralized and was en route to the burial grounds. The weather wasn't being too cooperative and the pallbearers were slipping and sliding as they tried to make their way up a steep hill in the mud. The storm was still brewing around them. Umbrellas had turned inside out, and raincoats were flapping in the breeze. They were about one third of the way up the hill when suddenly lightning began cracking all around, and it began raining like cats and dogs.

Shortie just happened to be on the heavy end. The pallbearers struggled on making their way about halfway up the mountain, when Shortie could bear his burden no more. The coffin slipped, Shortie fell and the coffin began sliding back down the way they had just come.

In the valley below was a small town, and a drug store just happened to be located in the middle of downtown. Ole Doc had slid open his french doors and turned on his ceiling fan against the intense heat and humidity that had built up before the storm. That pine box slid right down that mountain and into the front door of the drugstore. When it came to a halt against a counter, the lid popped open, the straps broke and the ole fellow sat up as if he were looking over the prescription counter.

Doc looked over his gold spectacles and asked, "Can I help you?"

The reply, "Yes sir, can you give me something to stop this coffin?"

Keep On Keepin' On

The only place I could get customers was from my competition, because there were not that many new people moving into town. I had a fellow call me one evening just before closing time. He said that he was glad he had caught me and that he was at a party with a lot of people. He reminded me he had been to the doctor that day, and I had filled a prescription for him. I told him I remembered and asked how could I be of help.

"Well," he said, "this might be a funny question to ask, but can I have a cocktail with this medicine?"

Jokingly I said, "Throw away the medicine and take the drink."

He turned around and told the whole crowd what I had said. The next day my business grew by twenty new customers. At some time or another they all told me they had been at that party.

It's tough being an independent pharmacy owner, trying to compete with the big boys, running it by yourself and making an effort to get established. My motto was, "keep on keeping on, and don't ever look back." I was working an average of a hundred hours every week through the first three years. To keep my sanity I turned to what my daddy had taught me to enjoy and appreciate when I was back home growing up. God's wonderful world of the great outdoors became my crutch. It was almost impossible for me to get out to fish or hunt, which I really enjoyed. So I decided to promote those that did get to participate by encouraging them to come by to show off their kill or brag on what they caught. It wasn't long before I had a wall full of pictures and a scrapbook of trophy snapshots. I began having contests and giving prizes for the catch of the month.

When I was able to join the crowd, I was like a bull in a new pasture. I was overjoyed to be one of the participants. I began writing articles for a new weekly paper called *The Griffin Gazette*. It was a challenge writing stories about my experiences of woods and waters and about other sportsmen. *The Gazette* could not afford to pay for my articles so I chalked it up to experience. I was sorry to see that paper fold and appreciated the many people who told me they had never missed any of my stories. Some had even read them to their children at the breakfast table.

I also had my own radio show interviewing other sportsmen and passing on a few stories about my own adventures. All my outdoor experiences were related to my business in some way. I loved to see kids get involved in field and stream enjoyment.

I have been an outdoor writer for twenty-five years and attribute my respect for Mother Nature to the few short years that I had the pleasure of learning from my father.

An Ounce of Prevention

If there is but one lesson I learned from all my years involved in the medical profession, it would definitely be, "An ounce of prevention is worth a pound of cure." Beginning in my second year of pharmacy school and throughout my entire life, I have taken the complete alphabet of natural vitamins from Alfalfa to Zinc. I have been blessed with wonderful health. I attribute this fact to my vitamin regimen.

Even today I have no need for wearing glasses. And all my life I have only had to visit the physician a couple of times. I did start annual checkups three years ago. I never miss my vitamins and some days take them twice. I have heard that if a person eats the right foods vitamins may not be necessary, but I don't know many people in our fast-paced world who really eat as they should. And all too often most of the minerals and vitamins in our foods are poured out in the pot liquor we

drain off after cooking. I have passed my belief in vitamins on to thousands, and many returned to thank me and report favorable results.
Money cannot buy your health, and I am a firm believer in maintaining
good health through nutritional supplements.

TELL IT LIKE IT IS

Is the Pendulum Swinging the Other Way?

The memories I have shared on these pages will always be a part of me, the good and the bad. And now that we have come to the end of my memory rainbow, there's something I must lay on the line. I have shared on these pages some stories of my upbringing and have endeavored to explain why certain ways of looking at life were a part of my culture. I've shared some reactions to events that happened to me in the early days of integration. Now I want to look a little at ways the southern winds are blowing today.

There seems to be a prevailing sense of animosity among many, which we are still being made to pay for the wrongs of our fathers. I feel that blacks should hear what many white people have to say, how it seems that there is a tendency in this day and time to overcompensate for the days when blacks were not treated, as they should have been. Not only have the days of equality for blacks come to the forefront, the pendulum now seems to be swinging back the other way, and there is a cry for equality for white folks.

Only three generations before me, my father's and mother's families owned slaves. It should be very easy to understand that a completely different type of relationship existed then between the master or owner and the slaves he had purchased. This was because the master felt since he had invested good money for them on the auction block, they belonged to him and he could do with them as he pleased. This must have been the mental frame of mind that caused the master to think he had the right to do anything he so desired with them, particularly the women. In that time blacks were not considered to be, nor were they treated like, human beings. In many cases slaves were treated more like animals.

While the master encouraged this, the older slaves also tried to ingrain into the minds of their children attitudes and ways they should behave toward the white folks. This is sadly depicted in Lillian Smith's book, *Strange Fruit*. She recounts a scene where a young slave boy has been beaten by his mama for talking *fresh* to a white girl. When her husband came home from work and saw Henry, swollen-faced and bleary-eyed, he demanded an explanation. He reprimanded his wife strongly for the beating she had given. They argued about this for some time and the final words she spoke in defense of the beating are astounding. She said, "He ain't good as white folks. I've got to learn him that. I gotta do it"

Not only did some of the white people feel this to be true, many of the colored people felt that way also. It took many years for this attitude to change and for acceptance to set in that we are all God's children. Now most people seem to be striving to live together until something comes along and tears down the building blocks of communication that both sides have erected. The O. J. Simpson trial was not good for race relations. It was very racial and did no good for any of us. Can you imagine how long the trial would have been had the media not made such a circus out of it? Certainly not as long as it was! A question being asked by many is, "Since O.J. was found to be innocent, why isn't there an ongoing investigation to see if they can catch the culprit?"

We try to get things on an even keel and along comes Freaknik! I wonder if the organizers of it ever give a thought to the problems and taxpayers' expense this event imposes on Atlantans. Or, is their mind only on pleasure and recognition and lining the pockets of a few? This type of fun and games retards the growing and acceptance process and knocks down a lot that has been built up.

Let's see what I mean by this. Freaknik is a method of showing younger generation's black power. There certainly has been very little visionary thought displayed pertaining to disruption of lives, and expense for a few days of pleasure. There are:

Police additions and protection	Cost money
Meetings for city government	Cost money
Closing of banks	Cost money
Closing of businesses	Cost money
Closing of eating establishments	Cost money
Diversion of traffic	Cost money
Operation cleanup	Cost money

Almost everything in the city seems to be placed in limbo. Productivity is automatically at a standstill. This whole scene becomes a liability to the City of Atlanta and in the long run costs the property owners through their taxes.

Recently I met a gentleman from Dallas, Texas who had the misfortune of flying to Atlanta on business during this year's Freaknik. He said that it was the mistake of his life. It not only cost this person hundreds of thousands of dollars, but it also cost his company a contract. He was caught up in traffic and unable to make his meeting. His potential customers assumed he wasn't interested. He was very unhappy about the situation and highly recommended that his company not buy the block of Olympic tickets they had planned to purchase. He just could not understand why the City of Atlanta could allow this to take place. It caused so many to change their everyday venues just to accommodate a couple of hundred thousand students out to have fun, if you can count lewdness, breaking into stores and blocking traffic fun.

There are many areas throughout the South that are geared toward handling mass vacationers without upsetting an entire metropolitan city. I love to have fun as well as anyone but not at the other fellow's expense.

Blacks have progressed and are taking over sports. Take a look at basketball, football, baseball and boxing. The only white majority you find is quarterbacks and pitchers, and the whites are gradually losing out on that.

When I was in high school, we had a 150 lb. line average in football. That wasn't too bad 'cause most of the other teams Valdosta played had the same. One by one the black boys were bussed and tokened into the white schools. Now the average line is almost double.

The basketball team I played on had maybe three guys that were a few inches over six feet. Today most of the players are closer to seven feet. You really have to be quick as lightening and highly skilled to become a pro or play on any team.

Blacks as a whole seem to be getting larger. Their size makes them extremely valuable in sports. Not many blacks have excelled in golf, tennis and swimming, but there are some blacks who are making a name for themselves in these areas, too. I have been told that back in the years of slavery, blacks were purposely crossbred in order to increase their size. Others say a diet of collard greens, pot liquor and cornbread was the main reason for their size. That doesn't seem likely, as this type of food is no longer the core of their diet and they still seem to be getting bigger and taller. I cannot even begin to talk about collard greens. I dislike the smell and even the name.

It has always been a belief that watermelon is a favorite with black people. Well, we have something good in common, because I also love watermelon. In fact, I have tried swimming with one under each arm, riding a bicycle with one hand on the handlebars and holding a watermelon with the other. I usually was looking over my shoulder to make sure farmer Brown wasn't after me. It was almost a rite of passage that we had to swipe at least one watermelon as we grew up. Anytime watermelon is served, I'm first in line.

In the 1960's the quota system was instituted. This is still a part of federal mandates today. In many cases blacks have been given jobs over better-qualified white people so that these quotas could be met. Now white people are saying it isn't right. As I was writing this, I heard on the news about eight white policemen and policewomen on the Atlanta force who had sued the city for what is termed reverse discrimination. The verdict was just handed down in favor of the white men and women who brought the suit. Do you see what I mean by the pendulum beginning to swing in the other direction?

When I worked hard labor in my uncle's concrete plant in Florida in the 1950's, I was paid $1.00 per hour. Even though I was in charge of 37 black men on the night shift who were paid $1.35 per hour, my uncle showed no favoritism.

I mentioned that our friend, James, removed his switchblade to protect my brother and me when he was babysitting. Most of the black boys then carried one in their pockets. During my growing up years, this was about as important a habit as putting on one's pants. Most of the problems back then were caused or at least aided by moonshine, but today there is the added stimulant of drugs at the root of many crimes. Today the *stobbens* of my younger years are almost a thing of the past, as pistols or Uzi's have taken the place of the switchblade.

What Goes 'Round Comes 'Round

In the 50's and 60's, sir and ma'am were caught up in the undertow of transition and blown away in the hot, dry, southern winds of change. However, I am hearing the return of these sounds of respect more and more, especially by blacks and whites in the South. Many times I hear it across the counter in eating establishments. I have heard it lately on *Montel* and *Oprah*. I recently heard a young white girl from Tennessee address Al Roper as "sir" on the *Today* show. On the same program Al Roper said, "Thank you, Sir" to Willard Scott for a compliment he had paid him.

When Bryant Gumble was on the *Today Show*, he was asked what his colleagues thought about the young kids of today not showing manners as well as they did in his day. He mentioned that courtesies were missing, i.e., Thank you, sir and ma'am and please. Someone said that maybe all this was because things just aren't as formal now as they used to be. Bryant then made a very astute reply, *"Please and Thank you start at home. I think manners should begin by the time a child is three years old."*

Children are slowly beginning to address their parents as they once did. Maybe things have run their full circle. I had a schoolteacher tell me that at the beginning of this school year, she had a couple of children who addressed her as ma'am. At the end of the school term, there were about ten or twelve in the class who addressed her that way. She said she did not ask this of any of the students, but somehow they discovered that they could catch more flies with honey.

I see many young white boys getting into the habit of eating with their hats on. The fad now is to wear them with the bill turned to the back. I cannot even imagine sitting down at a table to eat wearing a hat. In some cases parents may teach these kids better manners, but other kids are more of an influence. When my parents said no, I knew that was just what they meant, and I dared not go against what they said. I was recently eating in a restaurant where I heard one parent say no to the same question at least ten times and finally gave into the child's request. All this made me wonder who was really in charge of that household.

Maybe some white folks are guilty of sitting on their asses while blacks worked theirs off. We figured we were in charge and took for granted everything we had earned would remain as is. Blacks have gotten their acts together and polished up their goals. Most of us had been preconditioned and had black people stereotyped. I am sure that most colored people had Mr. Whitey stereotyped also.

Actually I have never seen anyone whose color was black. I've seen albinos and mulattos. I've seen people who were tan, brown and chocolate. The man who set the conveyor belt in motion at my Uncle's concrete plant came as close to being black as anyone I have seen.

Until lately, I had not heard the colored folks termed as black. The phrase African American also has come to the forefront. Lately I have heard the term Octoroon to describe a person who is one-eighth black. Some white folks have been surprised when they were claimed as kin by one of these octoroons. There were a lot of dark complected folks in South Georgia when I grew up. Mama always said, "Beauty is only skin deep." She advocated that what was inside a person was always more important than beauty on the outside.

When Eugene Talmadge was Governor of Georgia he was quoted as saying, "If God wanted us all one color, that would have been the way He made us. He certainly would not have made us black or white if it had been intended that we be one color." Many people say today that if the browning trend continues in America, we will one day all be one color.

I have been fascinated through the years at how the white and black women have tried everything they could do to change their color, reverse the process so to speak. With tanning beds and beaches, the white women seek to be brown. Some black women use bleach creams to appear whiter. And with all this comes the drive for perpetual youth. Some want to straighten their hair while others want theirs curled. There are those who want braided hair, corn rowed, pressed or ironed hair and bleaches or colors of almost any hue.

When I was a little boy in Valdosta, Ish and Sam, the two colored barbers in the Valdes Hotel, had requests from highfalutin white men to singe their hair. Ish or Sam would soak a long, cotton tipped applicator stick with a solvent. Then they would slowly comb the hair while singeing the ends. I have no idea why they did it, and I really don't believe they knew either. It was just something different and supposedly special. It looked to me as if they were trying to make their hair fuzzier like some black folks.

THERE IS PRIDE IN SEPARATE CULTURES

Sweet Doll

Fishing will always remain one of my very favorite things to do. On many occasions my wife, Judy, and I have enjoyed making some colored people happy by sharing with them our catch of the day. There is one very friendly black woman I particularly remember. She was round as a basketball, had puffy cheeks and chuckled every time she talked. She began setting up her chair next to our ramp and would be there when we returned from fishing.

She called Judy, Sweet Doll. And I can hear her now as she would say, "Lawsey me, Sweet Doll, you did it again." I could tell that Judy liked this title, and I once had a bakery decorate a birthday cake for her with the name Sweet Doll on it.

It has always seemed to me that the woods and waters were full of laughter. Anytime I am out of doors, I feel relaxed and more easy going. It was fun to share a string of fish with the black folks, who seemed appreciative and happy to get them. We had something in common there, because we all loved to catch and eat the fish.

It's a different story today. We meet the black fishermen in their bass boats out on the water. Another sign of progress, and that is good. But, there is also pride in separate cultures. We have bass clubs. There are also many clubs and tournaments that are just for the black folk. I think this is great.

The U.S. Would Be Dull Without the South

In the days when we had to go through a telephone operator to get a long distance call, their ethnic background was nearly always distinguishable by words such as "fo" to indicate for or four. Once in a while now, we might hear "poh-lice" and "dee-part-mint", and sometimes "ax" for ask, but for the most part it is difficult to distinguish. There are now more differences in regional dialects such as northerners and southerners, and with the diverse cultures in America, there is even a movement underfoot to establish a national language.

I have always been recognized as being a Southerner. It doesn't take a Yankee but a moment to know that my dialect has no verbal tones that resemble theirs. They even think that I sound funny. Once when I was a teenager, I caught a train and railed it up to Cincinnati to visit my brother who was attending the university there. His P.E. teacher adopted me during that week. Peg enjoyed taking me around the campus to meet her friends. When I spoke, everyone listened. I didn't realize that it was my dialect that swept them off their feet. I was treated to free meals and milk shakes thinking I had made a real hit with them. My balloon burst just a bit, when I found out that they just wanted to hear me talk.

I thought THEY talked funny. Anybody who would say "jeet" when they meant "did you eat" just didn't know how to speak. The person being asked the question would reply in some foreign language like, "Naw, jew?" I found that this meant, "No, did you?" I think they must have learned to talk fast like that because it was always too cold just to stand around and chew the fat. One good thing I learned on that visit was never to talk too fast7 for fear that I would sound like them—the Yankees.

My Aunt Eya taught me a saying, "Procrastination is the thief of time." I wasn't ever guilty of being a procrastinator. I just never did intend to get in a hurry, talking or otherwise.

Confucius told me when I was a boy, "He who takes his time gets the most," and I took Confucius at his word. Although I never really lived in the country, whenever I went there for a visit, I seemed to fit right in.

When I retired to live in the mountains of northeast Georgia, which may not exactly be the country, I found that people here don't get in too big of a hurry. A friend of mine told me I must have some country in me and reminded me of the saying, "You can take the boy out of the country, but you can't take the country out of the boy." The United States of America would be a dull place to live without all the beauty, the diversity of people and the colloquialisms found in the South.

The Scape Goat

When I recall the story of the policewoman in the drugstore, I remember that I had always called her by her first name, and she called me Dr. B. It had been the same throughout my life. Never had I called any colored woman "Mrs." As one dear old friend, Auntie, used to say, "It just bees dat way." We got along beautifully in our morning hellos. Across the pharmacy counter, my professional manners and her response were always friendly. We had no problems. She did a beautiful job looking after and protecting the children at the school. All the colored people I knew had always been addressed by their first name unless I claimed kin, and then I called them Auntie or Uncle. To be expected to change twenty-five or more years of tradition was hard.

I had earned the title of Doctor by being a member of the medical team. Back then it was customary to show respect by dealing out the term Doc. I often heard "old Doc in the corner pharmacy" or Doctor. I did not require anyone to do this. It was just a term of respect.

To look at this in a different perspective, the woman obviously felt she had earned the right and respect to be called Mrs. However, I assumed she very well could have been prodded into feeling this way.

Thus, the ground rules of the future began unfolding. Unlike participating in one of the games of chance in a Las Vegas casino at MGM where the intent was to make me comfortable and happy while losing, suddenly and forcefully changes were demanded and expected. Yes, this policewoman was married and legally had the right to be addressed as Mrs. Her husband owned and successfully operated a dry cleaning business with both black and white customers trading with him. He had graduated from an all black high school and later attended The Tuskegee Institute in Alabama. While attending college he excelled in track and was nicknamed Racehorse. To further indicate that black leaders were later accepted, this man was elected in the 1970's to become the first black Mayor of Griffin, Georgia and was even re-elected for a couple of terms.

But back in the early days of integration, his wife was in the pharmacy several times a week. She was a good customer. To my knowledge, no saleslady, cosmetician, owner of the store or the other pharmacist who had been employed there for many years had ever addressed her as Mrs. I felt that she knowingly selected me on that particular day to call my hand at this, since other prescriptions had been written by the same doctor and filled by me in the past with no recognition of Mrs. on her labels. Was it festering inside of her, or could it have been a well-planned strategy that she had developed with others?

A white gentleman from deep South Georgia was about as southern as it got. By this time Florida had begun to be populated by many people from the North who didn't have southern traditions so deeply ingrained. It seemed that I had the credentials and credibility for becoming The Scape Goat. I felt that one of the first cannon blasts of the new era was fired at me that day in the pharmacy, and like a concussion it opened my eyeballs. There were no volleys, as I had nowhere to aim my shots in return. I had been completely unaware that I was the enemy. I had to just sit down and remain there, with so much of my heritage and culture sinking in quicksand as these changes began to develop.

Strong Winds of Discontent

I cannot say for certain but believe it was Socrates who once said, "I count that man idle who can better himself." I had been too busy getting established to be idle. Working long hours every day had kept me from feeling any grass growing under my feet and apparently had kept me from feeling the strong, southern winds of discontent that were blowing among the colored folks. In some cases people whom I had counted as friends suddenly became hostile and demanding.

The NAACP became an architectural organization providing a well-planned course for instilling the feelings that a better world was needed and was attainable if they just followed the blueprints. As the name states, it was for the advancement of colored people. Perhaps the name should now be changed to NAABP because of the preference for the term Black, or should it be NAAAAP for the advancement of the African American people.

I'm sure if my father were still around, his viewpoints would never ever change. It seemed that overnight I was confronted with a completely different attitude from the colored race. "Do unto others" had a different ending; it became "before they do unto you."

Changes were demanded, expected and often came about while the white man was trying to sleep. All of a sudden the rules had been changed. As if they had been led like sheep to pasture, the term Black Power began blaring over the South. Their goal was to take over the government, police and fire departments, get into politics and integrate neighborhoods. Eventually everything would be under black control. People were told that if they registered to vote, then they could control the black vote. The goal was not to choose the best man for any job, be he black or white. The goal was black power. Promote the parts of black history that were okay. Erase the parts of black history that they no longer wanted known. Do away with some of the wonderful books that depict black culture such as *Old Black Joe* or *Little Black Sambo*. Have you tried to get a copy of the wonderful movie, *Song Of the South*? You can't get it.

I should have never had to go through the hell I did to protect my business. It mattered not how much I had done to help my colored clientele. It mattered not that many of the nights I had returned to the store for emergencies were for blacks. Because their ancestors had been treated unfairly by some of my ancestors, anyone who was white was expected now to pay.

It got to where I could not even go out and collect some of the debts owed to me by so many colored people. I took pepper spray along. But one day I needed to try and repel a dog who came running, barking and growling at me. I had the spray nozzle turned the wrong way and sprayed myself in the face. I must have been a funny sight as I danced around, blinded by my own hand, just waiting for Bruno to take a plug out of my leg or rear.

Persecution Just Ain't Right

I don't believe it is ever right for any race to persecute the other. It wasn't right for my ancestors, nor is it right today when the persecuting is being done by the blacks.

Integration was a historical revelation that unfolded like the petals of the Cherokee Rose, Georgia's state flower. It took about seventy-five years for the first rumblings of integration to come across the South.

When abolition of slavery transpired and the blacks were set free, some hit the road, while others realized that it hadn't been so bad after all. It could be worse. Still other blacks remained on the plantations, with work and a roof over their heads. There was a difference, though. Now they could leave if they so desired.

Cries and demands for integration began during the 50's and 60's, and have continued with legislation, mandates and quotas that mark almost everything one does today.

The racial waters were muddied by only a select few of each race. Disturbances and unrest developed, and over time this led to violence, and hatred.

Signs of the Times

In the period prior to World War II, billboards were erected across the South that read:

—In North Carolina: The Blackest Earth—The Whitest People.
—In Georgia: (The N. word)—don't let the sun set on your ass in White County.
—In Alabama: Many varieties of the same.

What caused this hatred, animosity and resentment?

There were many songs, sayings and jokes that sprung up during this span of time. These were mostly displayed in the northern areas of these states that, for the most part, Negroes had no inclination to inhabit. A friend of mine who was born and raised in northern Georgia saw her first black person at the age of ten when riding through Valdosta on the way to Florida with her parents.

The southern sections of most southern states had far more productive farmlands than the northern parts, and people settled there to raise
their families and survive the times. These people were easy going, busy
making a living and welcomed help with their farming or sharecrop-
ping. When colored folks migrated through the upper state areas, they
were harassed and, if they were lucky, were only run out of town.

A dear friend in the state of Rhode Island recalled the first time he
saw a colored boy was in a carnival. You could purchase three baseballs
for ten cents, throw them and try to trip a paddle that would let the boy
fall into a tub of water.

Another friend from New Jersey said he remembered a black family
moving into a house in a neighborhood in his town. The next day a
Borough Hall truck came, packed them all up again and moved them to
the next county.

Things Were Tough All Over

Things were tough all over. No matter where the Negro went, it was
hard to be accepted. If kinfolk were located in any particular area, then
they would try to join them. In many towns this would be across the
tracks or on a farm.

During this time there were very few facilities or accommodations
for colored people. In most courthouses and public buildings, there
were separate rest rooms and water fountains marked "White Only" and
"Colored". I am sure it was tough to locate a restaurant or a room to
rent for sleep when they traveled.

In some ways World War II can be looked on as a blessing in disguise
for colored people. There was very little discussion about race during
the heat of a battle at a war zone. Although barracks were still segre-
gated, there were many colored men who fought and died in defending
their country and winning the war.

These veterans returned from service and had the opportunity to earn a few years of college due to the G.I. Bill. Most entered predominantly black colleges just as the white men and women went to the white schools.

Maybe this also was the beginning of the blacks realizing that just being free did not give them equality. They began to feel that they were not receiving the same opportunities. They wanted to gain entrance in the state owned schools, especially since their people had also helped to win the war. They had a good point, but because many of my generation were not convinced that change even needed to be made, they certainly did not want to be forced, pushed and made to make these changes overnight.

Back of the Bus

Blacks became well organized and planned for The Movement to the nth degree. This began by word of mouth, gained recognition and was picked up by the media. Everywhere newspapers, radio, theaters and television picked up on this unrest and in some cases even added to it. This was *big news*, and increased attention meant increased sales or circulation. Any story was developed to its fullest.

The NAACP and other groups aimed at the betterment of colored people commanded respect and got attention. Supposedly non-violent marches seemed to spring up overnight. Most everyone assumes that the marches originated in Alabama. Actually, they began at the back of the bus. The day that only a few gained enough courage to refuse the seats in the back of the bus was the start of an avalanche that rolled down the mountain.

From there it spread like a contagious disease, from rest rooms, fountains to restaurants. For a short time movie houses allowed colored people to sit in the balconies. When they could not be controlled from spilling drinks over the rail, popping bags and dropping popcorn, then the owners gave up and decided—if you can't beat 'em, then let's join 'em.

Soon the schools were integrated and then later, in order to meet federally mandated quotas, busing began which at some times was ridiculous.

There is a saying, "Money talks, but it never gives itself away." Token integration of high class, white residential areas began. I had an aunt and uncle in Miami, Florida who had just invested their life savings in a beautiful new home there.

When the first black family moved in next door, the value of their new home dropped fifty percent. They took their loss and moved to the West Coast. This movement destroyed real estate investments throughout the South.

As white families moved out of the cities, black families soon followed, and then white families moved out even further. This became known as the white flight. Attendance at many private schools grew, as some of the wealthier families enrolled their children there in order to prevent attendance at public schools that now included blacks. Real estate values in some areas dropped overnight, and then black people could pick that property up for a song.

The black race did an outstanding job in a very brief period of time. They were well programmed. This feat would never have gotten off the ground if it had begun in the thirties. No one would have ever contemplated a boycott back then. You would have been out of your mind to lie down in the street. Anyone assuming to do so would have found that the Midas touch wasn't even around then. Things would have been quite different in the early days of the 20th century.

The Time Was Ripe

But their timing was just right. Blacks made much more progress than the white folks in this period of time. Someone said they really didn't have much to lose and everything to gain and should be recognized for their well-coordinated movement.

White folks did pave the way. So why not give them a little credit? Where did it all come from for you to just come along and demand a share? It may not have been the way the black people wanted for a beginning, but they soon overcame that.

Since I was born in the South and lived all my life there, I had a seat on the fifty-yard line to witness all of the players and each quarter of the game. I began to notice that when colored folks made their move from the farms to the cities, the farmers were left in deep manure. A fellow from New England said that when World War II began there was a dire need for factory and shipyard workers. So they began busing field hands from southern farms up the coast to work in the factories. When the War was terminated, everyone assumed that their workers would return to the farms. This was not the case. Many elected to remain where the money was coming in faster than they had ever dreamed. After a few years, they began returning to the South and pointing out to those who were still around that there was more to life than the drudgery of farm work.

Some were happy and satisfied with their lives, while others grabbed hold of the line that life would give them something for nothing. This was proof of an old saying, "Show me just one leader, and I shall show you ten thousand followers."

By demanding change and continuing to harp on the inequality of the slave years, suddenly it seemed as if every part of the white man's life was geared to atoning for their ancestors' transgressions. It soon became clear that equality was changing to supremacy. It seems to me that black supremacy is just as wrong as white supremacy!

Hopefully the leaders didn't push crossing the race lines. Really there was no need, as it was getting a foothold by itself.

The Soul of the City

Attitudes toward the white people now seem to be more of a "gotcha-back," and it's our turn now. Let's erase anything that has to do with telling all of the southern history. Tell only that which puts the white man in a bad light. Keep pushing, prodding, changing and taking over, and even get in there and change the state flag.

Restoration of the Margaret Mitchell House had been delayed twice in Atlanta. This was done by arsonists. Prove to me that blacks didn't do it. *Gone With The Wind* represents the soul of the city and depicts southern heritage. Why was the fire that destroyed the Margaret Mitchell House allowed only to receive an honorable mention on television news? They casually said it might have been racial. If the beautiful Ebenezer Church Reverend King preached in was destroyed, I don't believe it would be overlooked. No, the news media would thrive—lest we forget.

The media has been rife with stories about the burning or torching of churches across the South lately. It really depends on which television station you watch or which paper you read as to what is happening. In addition to the black churches that have been burned, there have also been white churches burned during the same time. But again and again you will find that this is rarely, if ever, mentioned, and the phrase, "racially oriented" is frequently stated as the cause of the fires at the black churches.

According to the television program *Cross Fire*, there actually have been more white churches torched. But again, these stats have been swept under the carpet by many. When this was mentioned on *Cross Fire*, Jessie Jackson, who was one of their guests, continuously kept talking and trying to prevent attention being brought to this fact. The commentator tried five times to question the fact that not only black churches, but white ones as well, were being torched and burned before Jessie Jackson would acknowledge him. The media did show an inter-racial church, with members of both races sharing the grief of a black minister. Again and again these fires are said to be racially motivated or oriented. Maybe I am wrong in the way I look at all this, but it seems to me that they could well be religiously motivated.

HERITAGE

Diversity

We are constantly being bombarded with news of Black History. Only good things are reported, of course. I don't understand why people feel that the black race should be individualized. We are all different. My wife is French American. I am Scot American. A dear friend of mine is part Indian or as they now say, Native American. My neighbor is Italian American. What if we all pushed the issue and asked, "What about me? Tell my story!" There had to be some injustices done to all people at some time or another. How about every ethnic culture asking to let folks "know about my heritage?" There would be no time for bringing the news because of the time it took to recognize all our ancestral background.

I am proud of my heritage and will take the bad along with the good. Every race, nation, and family has events in their history that one would prefer not to have happened. But they did, and they are and will always be a part of their history.

It seems that a great many people in all ethnic groups prefer to live and worship among their own. Forced integration, quota systems and such would not be necessary if they were left alone to make their own decisions. Take a good look at a listing of some of the finest colleges in the South, and you will find Morris Brown, Spelman and Morehouse in Atlanta. These are predominately black establishments, and while they are open to all races, they are prime examples of the desire of the black race to have colleges of their own, for their own. The millions of dollars Bill Cosby donated to one of the colleges in the Atlanta University system weren't given to benefit the white folks, of course. No, they were given for the improvement of the black race now and in the future. There are constant pleas in the media for money to be given to the Black College Fund, with the implication that this money is tagged only for blacks. We also hear of the Miss Black America Beauty Contest—this title specifically does not include other ethnic groups.

Freedom of Choice

While all churches are now open for integration, why is it that most of the black race chooses to attend a church that is predominately of their own ethnic origin? I guess it is for the same reason that the Jewish people choose to attend their synagogues, and most of the Korean Americans choose to attend a predominately Korean church. The last place that integration doesn't seem to be working is in our churches. I wonder why. It could be a custom, but I think that it is cultural selection. Maybe just knowing that one is free to go anywhere he or she chooses is all that some people want. And, with that knowledge, in most cases individuals prefer to live and worship with those whose ethnic background is similar.

There are Jewish, Negro and Caucasian cemeteries. There are undertakers and funeral homes that, while available to all, cater most specifically to blacks or to whites. There are usually white preachers for funerals of the white folks, and there are usually black preachers for the funerals of the black folks. Marriage vows and baptismal rites are sacred, and it is evident we all tend to choose those of our own culture and heritage.

There really seems to be a cultural division and sacred ground for us all. Why is that? Is this something passed down from our forefathers?

Many Jewish people would like to return to their homeland, Israel, so I have been told. Blacks can't even bear the thought of returning to Africa. They would prefer that their heritage come to them. While other ethnic groups are proud of their heritage, there seems to be more of an attitude of, we are now Americans. We are all in this boat together, so let's make the best of this Country for ALL of us.

A lot of feces has been forced upon the multitudes by only a minority. There was objection. People had no idea what had hit them. Instead of letting us all live and let live and be proud of our culture, there is a movement afloat to see that we all accept one culture, and that is the black culture. I suppose it is hard for the black race to have the same point of view as me. After all, I was the one lying on the floor trying to protect my investments from the black men out there looking in and keeping me there. This wasn't something happening to my ancestors, this was happening directly to me!

Oath Without Prejudice

I had taken an oath to take care of the sick, and I certainly always abided by this with absolutely no prejudice. So how do you imagine I felt when I was on the receiving end of unwarranted transgressions?

Time heals all wounds it is said. But for some reason, it seems that it serves the black race to keep the wounds of wrongdoing by our ancestors open and festering so that they never heal. When I finally felt secure enough to leave my store at night, go home and get a peaceful rest, I was able to take some time and turn around and get a good look at what was happening to my town. I saw just what the black man was doing and the changes that were being made mostly by force.

I looked at the journey that the black man has traveled. I also thought about how many times after midnight I had returned to my pharmacy to aid a black family's emergency. And when I had the courage to look over my bookkeeper's reports, I noticed that the past due accounts were by far those of the black race. Why then, with my helpfulness and thoughtfulness, was I being targeted with hatred?

Christopher Darden has written a book about his life and some of his experiences surrounding the trial of O. J. Simpson. There is one statement that jumps out from the pages of that book, "I owe it to my society to marry a black woman and have black children." During the O. J. trial, you will remember the media tried to make Christopher and Marcia Clark appear to be closer than friends or co-workers. I guess this was to add an element of spice and keep those ratings up.

As I watch television talk shows, I've noticed that black women have a distinct resentment for black men who have crossed the racial line and are dating or marrying outside their race. It is as if they cannot tolerate or begin to understand the reasoning behind it.

It brought a sense of dismay to me when I recently saw a black boy sitting between a couple of white girls bragging on the fact that both were pregnant by him. He also let everyone know that he had been with a dozen more white girls. Part of this dismay is my own cultural shock, and part of it is the flaunting of the breakdown of morals.

As I reflect on my upbringing, it is very hard for me to swallow and not feel utter resentment for this scene filling up my television screen. At least I have the means of changing channels, but the image remains in my mind.

I definitely am not trying to be controversial. I am only being frank and sincere about all of us as human beings.

Oprah appeared to really enjoy the show she aired on Octoroons. They are one-eighth Negro according to Webster's Dictionary. It was obvious that she got a real kick out of having the so called *white folks* discovering that somewhere down the line there had been an interracial relationship that had been kept quiet for a few generations. You can imagine the surprise on those white southerners faces as that information was revealed.

Respect Can't Be Forced, And Love Can't Be Mandated

Communication has become the way of life, but more and more frequently it has become the norm for the black point of view to be expressed. Everyone else must sit back and listen. It has been a revelation.

All of the other ethnic and diverse cultures have stories too, but it is as if all that is being swept under the carpet with a "who cares attitude." The melody of our heritage lingers on in our minds and in our hearts but has become like a taboo subject.

There really are two sides to every story and in order for us to understand each other, work and live together, other voices need to be heard. It is as if strong tornado-like winds have swept across the nation and particularly across the South, blowing away the voices from the white man's past.

I believe many blacks today realize that much has also been forced upon them. It's almost like deciding to serve on a committee, thinking it would involve only a night or two a month, and finding out that you were needed at meetings several times a week. They got more than they bargained for, and only a few came out smelling like a rose. If more blacks had been in on the decision making, I wonder if there would be a different story. Many quite possibly would have preferred to accomplish their goals in their own way.

It seems that the North had some type of love for the Negro race as a whole. Maybe it was only in trying to understand. The South slowly developed their love for the individual over a longer period of time.

Love for anyone cannot be brought on by force. It must be slowly created and gradually accepted. It is like traveling uphill on a long, long road.

Feelings among people must be mutually sincere and deep from the heart. Love and understanding cannot be mandated. There must be trust for each other in order to develop a lasting relationship. This cannot be dealt out to the players like a deck of cards.

People of all races feel a sense of pride in their heritage and culture, and rightly so. During the past fifty years, the black race has more to toot the whistle about than anyone else I know. They have accomplished more during this era toward standing up and being counted for than at any other time. But, when someone is taught right and wrong during their stages of development, and those tenets are ingrained in the very core of one's system, it is close to impossible to ferment instant change.

I was taught to "Seek ye first the kingdom of God; Honor my father and mother along with Love thy neighbor." My parents controlled the switch, the direction and the speed for which I traveled down the yellow brick road of life.

When I came of age, my parents pushed me out of the nest, as it certainly should have been. They knew that I had the foundation for becoming a responsible and contributing adult.

But, the deep-seated love that I possess for my Mother and Father developed over a period of time, not overnight. I always cared about them, but it took time for love to develop. And then there was no way of placing a gauge on my love for them and saying, "Okay, you can only love them this much."

I knew that I would have no way to pay them back for what they had given to me. They didn't want any paybacks. They only wanted success and happiness for their sons. We were thankful for our heritage, and when we left home, there were many more lessons to learn as we added to and developed that which was instilled in us.

When my mother died, she had left a letter for each of her sons. She asked that we not be too busy to remain in close contact with each other like she and her sister Etta had done. Thankfully, I can say that Jimmie and I have remained close and take time to communicate.

We, ALL, Are Human Beings

It seems to me that the black people have been so busy fighting for equality, getting established and demanding what was denied for many years, that there is one fact that has been forgotten. That is—*WE* are also human beings.

It was Harry Belafonte who said, "If we can only understand these perceptions." Mr. Webster defines perceptions as, "any insight or knowledge that we can acquire." I think we must all be patient, and that we all should make a more concentrated effort to gain a better understanding for each other. This should apply to the black people just as much as the whites.

I, for one, am fully aware of the road that has been traveled by the black race. History books, documentaries and article upon article have been written telling of this journey. I can see more clearly now that there **is** pride in separate cultures. The path or direction taken from this point on can be one of extreme pride, if it is handled with care and with the understanding that there are others living in this great country of ours.

How about reciprocating, taking a look at the heritage of others and trying to understand?

We Southerners did develop a love and trust for so many of the black race. And they gained the same respect for us. Listen closely to Martin Luther King's great speeches and sermons as he talked about his dreams. How many times did he include the words, "It's not the color of your skin but the content of your character." That is food for thought by everyone.

Many times I have said that memories are made of fulfilled dreams. They do last a lifetime, and you can't take one's memories away from them. They linger on, all the good times and the bad. Sure, we all prefer to remember only the good times, but ignoring the bad cannot change the past. Dreams leave off where memories take over. Just as Reverend King was mainly speaking to the colored people of their Rights, he was not negating the Rights of ALL men.

God works in mysterious ways. Leprosy was a disease during the Biblical times. We are told that AIDS originated in Africa. Why then did it wait for an eternity, evolve and make its sudden appearance now? God controls our lives. He will always be the Power. We are admonished so many times over and over again to live right. Why can't we all try to get along together, because life is too short.

Change Begins Within

The older one gets, the more you come to realize that life is always full of change. Some changes are certainly for the best, while others are hard to understand. We often tend to cling to memories and talk about the good ole days. There is reason for every one of us to be proud of the contributions our diverse cultures have made to this earth. There is also reason for us to look back and regret some of the contributions that are a part of history. Wouldn't it be great if we could all take a brush and paint out the parts we find distasteful? That's not possible, because what we are now is a sum total of ALL that has gone before. We live in the here and now and hopefully strive to learn from mistakes and leave this earth a little better than we found it, not just for the blacks or the whites, but for *everyone*.

The quietus has been put on some wonderful songs that brought only happy memories to my generation. I miss singing and hearing songs like *Shortnin' Bread* and *Sleep Kentucky Babe*. That kind of song brings only happy memories; in fact, my mother used to sing me to sleep with *Sleep Kentucky Babe*. It is extremely hard for me to understand why the black people find them so oppressing and distasteful.

Sunday night radios were tuned in millions of homes across the nation to *Amos and Andy,* not because of poking fun at the black race. No, rather because of the joy and laughter (not at, but with). When I cuddled up in Mama's lap to hear stories like *Little Black Sambo*, it was because I enjoyed hearing about his adventures. It's odd, but those songs, stories and radio programs stand out in my memory as treasured experiences. I always thought of the colored people who lived around me as being happier than anyone else I knew. Singing these songs and reading these stories somehow let me have a little share of their happy-go-lucky spirit, too.

One of the greatest movies I remember seeing was *Song Of The South*. My heart, and I am sure the hearts of millions of people, was filled with love for dear ole Uncle Remus as he walked along with the bluebirds singing *Zip A Dee Do Dah*. Movies like that simply must be better for us than the trash that comes across our airways and movie screens today.

Most of the children of today have no idea of what I am talking about, because these sounds have been silenced. But their grandparents haven't forgotten. About the only thing left is Aunt Jemima on the pancake box. Just looking at her happy face says that there is something good in that box, and I'm not really sure whether that is still around.

Out of sheer curiosity I took the time to conduct an unofficial survey involving people the ages of baby boomers or above. I covered several hundred folks from Miami on up the seaboard to Maine. There were a couple of pertinent questions that I asked. The first was not too serious, but it was very important to me. First, have you ever sung a few courses of *Mammy's Little Baby Loves Shortnin Bread*? Next, were there ever any Negro children in any of your classes in any of your years of education?

The answer to both questions was always the same, Yes. We sang *Shortnin' Bread*, or at least I know the song, and No, to the Negroes in the classroom. A lot of the northerners said, "We had our own schools. We didn't see very many of them up our way."

I personally was in school for nineteen years, and there was never a black person in any of my classes, nor in any of the churches I attended.

Recently I had the pleasure of participating in a game of chance at the MGM Grand in Las Vegas. It was really big time, and I assumed that it was way out of my league. I knew that it certainly wasn't like the friendly games of poker with which I was acquainted.

My wife had signed me up for this poker game, as she was tired of hearing me say that I really missed the game. So seated at the table, we had at one time a dealer from Persia. At his side was a Chinese lady. She was an excellent player and casually asked where each of us was from. The Jewish fellow next to me was Sy. He was from Boca Raton, Florida. He was a very nice man who had at one time owned the property across from the MGM. Next was a black man from Chicago, another from Texas, one from California, the Philippines and Mexico and so on 'til everyone had answered the lady's request. She turned to me, and I said, "Georgia."

She said, "So am I."

And I replied, "Small world, isn't it?"

Meanwhile, I donated the first evening to the cause and broke even the second. When the dad of Atlanta Braves pitcher, David Maddux, became my dealer for the third evening before I had to catch a plane and return home, I won fourteen out of the next seventeen deals. I left happy. And as the plane was cruising over the Grand Canyon, I had time to reflect on the fact that I had just participated at an international poker table. I didn't consider race, color or creed. We were all there to enjoy the evening and, hopefully, to win. I was more concerned about protecting my interests than who was playing the game with me. No one had forced me to participate. I just walked in, chose my seat and had fun with all those around me.

COMPASSIONATE
UNDERSTANDING

The Dust Has Almost Settled

When the next generation makes its appearance, I hope all of this ethnic pushiness and frustration will be caught up in the undertow of time and washed out to sea. Those warm southern winds will have blown away almost any vestige of these memories. It's just like wee-weeing in the sand. There will be no evidence of where it has gone.

Respect was taught on both sides of the tracks. It was instilled in us like breathing in and out, with no questions asked. I am positive that most of the wonderful colored folks that I have had the pleasure of knowing during my life never questioned it either. These things that were just taken for granted and accepted now seem to be flowing like a river out to sea.

I only want this generation of black people to be able to perceive and understand the changes as seen from both sides of the tracks. There needs to be a compassionate understanding for all mankind and consideration given to the feelings of others.

I only speak for myself and mean no harm to anyone. I represent no one. I take full responsibility for the thoughts I have shared on these pages. I have only tried to explain my feelings, their formation and the way I traveled and reacted through the changes of life that were forced upon my generation by the black people. This will have repercussions for generations to follow.

Perhaps by walking a mile or two in my shoes, the white man's viewpoint might be easier to understand.

As I said, there is no doubt about where the Movement came from and why it came about. My generation of white folks and I served as stepping stones for these changes in so many ways. The dust has almost settled. It seems to me that past injustices have been atoned for, and today we don't have to answer to anyone—except our God.

But we must now be careful of those who keep trying to push the pendulum until it swings completely in the other direction. We must continue to find ways to live and work together in harmony. We must find a way for the equality we share to mean just that. And having attained as level a playing field as life will give to anyone, we must now work to earn whatever recognition is due to each and every individual.

Epilogue

WHO PAID THE PRICE?

Of course, you did.
Your ancestors had on the shackles, the leg irons,
the ball and chain.

It really wasn't you that suffered the pain
of crossing the sea in the hole of a ship,
caged like animals.
Separated from families with nothing to gain.

The villain set them up on the auction block,
and the master paid his fee.

But when you decided to climb the mountain
and rushed to get to the top,
one of the stones you stepped on
could have been me.

It's time now to forgive and forget,
and begin a new chapter in our
His-to-ry.

The End

About the Author

W. Everett Beal has written over 400 articles for magazines and newspapers. Everett is currently a member of The Georgia Writers Inc., Southeastern Outdoor Writers Assoc, and the Georgia Outdoor Writers Assoc, where he is a former president. He has appeared in radio shows, television programs and movies. He was born and raised in Valdosta, Georgia and after eight years of college moved to Griffin, Georgia to practice as a registered pharmacist where he owned and operated a pharmacy. He later owned another pharmacy in Gainesville, Georgia. After retiring as a pharmacist, he and his wife, Judy, opened a Christmas Shop in Dillard, Georgia and lived at Sky Valley for 16 years. They returned to Griffin.

The author lived and breathed every moment of *Southern Winds*. It was compiled on top of the mountain, in the sand by the sea and in the air and will stand the winds of time.